Margaret Wynn
908 Merion Square Rd.
Gladwyne, PA 19035

D1479341

Table for One

ALSO BY CHRISTINA HOLBROOK

All the Flowers of the Mountain

Table for One

STORIES

CHRISTINA HOLBROOK

Published by SUNROOM STUDIOS
Dillon, Colorado
Manufactured in the United States of America
ISBN
Paperback 979-8-9861488-4-7
Ebook 979-8-9861488-5-4

Cover and interior design by Ashley Prine
Cover image and interior illustration credits: Shutterstock: front cover, I, 118 © sini4ka; back cover snake © knstartstudio; 1, 4, 11, 93, 109 © Olga Rai; 7 © NikVector; 32 © CoolVectorStock; 39 © Valenty; 41 © Olga Khinevich; 43 © Tetiana Yurchenko; 45 © Haali; 55, 91 © Luckyrizki; 73 © NadzeyaShanchuk; 87 © Essl; 89; © BUCKLEY_S; 99, 111 © Derplan13; 103 © WinWin artlab; 107 © Fagreia

Disclaimer

Table for One is a work of fiction. Names, characters, businesses, places, events, locales, and incidents are either the product of the author's imagination or used in a fictitious manner. Any resemblance to actual persons, living or dead, is purely coincidental.

With gratitude to my husband, Alan

She wanted more than anything else in the world *to know*.

To possess and be possessed.

—from "Thief"

Contents

Table for One

Commencement

Each of them is given a dark robe to wear. A bulky chrysalis. Or a magician's cape, behind which they are already changing.

The two sit down together. She remembers sleepovers at his house, and how later she could have talked to him on the phone all night.

Now he shouts too-loud jokes to friends, as if it's not really the end. She clasps her hands, beginning to look away, to look ahead. Then it's her turn to rise and walk to the podium. Suddenly light, expectant.

He holds on to her empty chair.

Her robe flutters around her like wings.

Table for One

You check into the hotel near Dupont Circle, in DC. Gathered around the fireplace in the parlor, cocktail drinkers trade political gossip, while a twisty staircase leads to your guest room on the second floor. Splashed across the ceiling, a colorful mural displays the underside of a rowboat surrounded by ripples of blue water. As you stare up from the bed, a painted fishing line—an elongated question mark—appears to descend directly toward you. You could be under water, like a frog or a fish or (you prefer to think) a mermaid.

When you go down for dinner, the hostess asks, "Table for one?" She scans the packed dining room. "Do you mind eating at the bar?"

Not at all. You won't have to wait as long for a drink.

Seated, with no companion as a distraction, you look over the menu. It's November and oysters are in season. Why not indulge your desires? You smile at the hazel-eyed bartender and he holds your gaze long enough for you to feel pleasure at this flirtatious overture. Then you order a dozen oysters—*actually, make that two dozen*—and a bottle of sauvignon blanc. After all, your first

3

appointment, at the National Gallery, is not until 11 o'clock the next morning.

Once, dining solo in Zurich, in a hotel restaurant well above your pay grade though not your employer's expense account, you selected truite au bleu. To your horror, the trout was gutted while alive. But the dish was French; for fear of exposing a squeamish lack of sophistication, you blanched and said nothing.

Another lone woman asked if she could join you. When it came your turn in the conversation to describe your work—*supervise the color accuracy and printing of art books*—her face betrayed incredulity.

"Museums send you around the world just to add a little more blue or subtract a little yellow?" she drawled.

Stated in that way, the preposterous truth made you both laugh out loud, gauche Americans.

Another time, while eating a forgettable meal at Heathrow and waiting for a connecting flight to the Frankfurt Book Fair, you were approached by an elderly gentleman who inquired if he might read your palm. It happened to be an uncertain juncture in your romantic life, so the offer seemed like a good idea. What your palm revealed: "You adore music and could not live without it."

You had never considered this before.

Also: "With high expectations in love, you will be continually disappointed."

Shouldn't fortune-tellers offer more optimistic predictions?

You determined the best course was to cultivate an appreciation for music.

As a result of frequent dinners alone in an Italian restaurant in your Manhattan neighborhood, you were asked by the head chef to join him with some of the staff at the "family table." *Grazie! So thoughtful!*

You shared the chef's rabbit stew, scooped up with hunks of bread seasoned with rosemary sprigs and garlic slivers. Later, he was kind enough to offer a tour of the downstairs wine cellar—a ruse in which you happily participated. A kissing session led to inadvertent entrapment in the freezer. Before passion turned to panic, a search party sent out by the overwhelmed cooks upstairs unlocked the heavy door. "I hope we're not disturbing you," remarked the world-weary sous-chef.

On a side trip to Chiang Mai during a printing assignment, you were eating outdoors—a cold, sweet soup with large mushrooms— and swatting mosquitoes. An attractive Australian girl pulled up to the restaurant on a motorbike. Your eyes met with the friendly recognition of single travelers and she immediately found her way to your table. Your expense account paid for both dinners.

What a coincidence it seemed when she bumped into you again on Ko Samui and drove you around the island on her bike.

Six months later, she showed up at your studio apartment, pregnant, and asked to move in.

I'm sorry, but there's hardly room enough for one!

For a long time afterward you wondered how, from Thailand, she had tracked you down to your apartment in New York.

The oysters are finished now, and so is the bottle of wine. You request that the charge be put on your hotel bill, and the bartender asks for your room number. He slides the receipt across the bar with his cell number written along the top and what is apparently his signature: Doctor Love.

I know that's not really your name, you inform him. Maybe he thinks you are drunk. So what if you are?

Back in your room, you lie in bed and stare up at that tantalizing fishing line. You decide to tap his number into your phone. You get it right on the third try.

Do you make house calls, Doctor?

Missed Flight

I feel better as soon as the car service arrives.

The driver is broad shouldered and turbaned. "Good morning, miss. My name is Balbir and I'll be taking you to the airport today."

He deposits my carry-on into the trunk, then opens the door for me. I slide inside the quiet comfort of the backseat. If Balbir has noticed I'm crying, he is too professional to remark on it.

At Kennedy, I walk past the surging line for Economy and head for the counter labeled BUSINESS CLASS, where I am one of two people checking in. It's not lost on me that the chauffeured town car and the solicitous attendants at the airport are privileges I experience because of my job. Outside of work, there are no such buffers to insulate me.

In the United executive lounge, I cradle a cappuccino in my hands; its warmth, like the orderly arrangement on the side table of *The Wall Street Journal*, *The Economist*, and *Business Week*, reassures and calms me. This airport is the gateway to my alternate life, one where I am not bone weary and scared but capable and worthy of respect.

In the life I've stepped out of temporarily, my husband, Reed, seethes at home over a careless remark of mine.

Sometimes, for no reason I can think of except to punish myself, I remember the irresistible attraction between us five years ago. Drinking martinis, sharing an occasional joint, we'd discussed our favorite Russian novels. His rebellious intelligence and literary bravado seduced me. Though I was just a junior financial analyst at the time, he'd seemed to find me worthy of his imagination and talent. His soul mate! Not, as I'd secretly feared, just a dull, plodding suit.

Last night, finishing up the dishes at the kitchen sink, I'd listened while Reed held forth with friends around his bong in our living room. "Do you realize that if I'd been in New York City on September 11, I would have been at Ground Zero, covering the story of that first plane crash for the magazine? Right when the towers collapsed!" He'd paused to let this theoretical near miss with catastrophe impress them. "Crazy, right?"

"But you weren't in New York," I'd pointed out from the kitchen. "You were in the Keys—remember? Fishing with Dave and T-Bone?"

He'd repeated this close-call boast so many times that I finally decided to speak up—because I *was* in New York that day, alone, as animal panic tore through every office in the city. I was the one who'd walked uptown after dark, among the cast-off shoes, the air filled with white dust and ghosts.

Later, he'd cornered me in the bedroom. "You were trying to ruin my story, weren't you? *Bitch*. You think you're such hot shit with your big investors and your fucking IPOs." His eyes flattened to fury. "You're still an office drone, Emily! Don't forget that. And you're jealous of me!"

I'd apologized, but not fast enough. He hadn't had an assignment in weeks. I should have kept my mouth shut. Who could I blame but myself for the rage and frustration that came at me in shock waves until morning?

At 6 a.m., finally spent, he'd groaned, "Gotta get some sleep. I'm turning my phone off. I'll talk to you next week."

When my car had arrived a few minutes later, I crept out with my roller bag, my carefully applied makeup an attempt to cover my exhaustion. I had twelve hours of travel ahead of me.

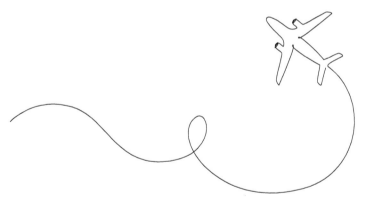

I look up at the departures board, see all the names of the different cities I could go to stacking and reshuffling: *Amsterdam. Tokyo. Dubai.* . . . On this trip my destination is London, but I can't help wondering *what if?* What if I took off to one of those other faraway cities? I close my eyes and linger in a place of nearly ecstatic release as I imagine just . . . *disappearing.*

"Em? I can't believe it's you!"

My eyes snap open at the sound of a voice I recognize. Tom, the guy I dated in college—so many years ago! For a moment I struggle to react. What a smart-ass I was back then: Ms. Honors Student, 100 percent sure that life promised me only happiness and success.

In the ten seconds it takes Tom to reach my seat, something inside me withers with shame at the person I've allowed myself to become. Bereft of self-respect. Lost. I sit up straighter and compose my expression into one of pleased surprise.

And I fool him. I'm good at that. With my expensive haircut, the sleek Armani blazer over jeans, my ability to bounce right into any conversation with intelligence and an engaging smile—I know how to appear as if I'm on top of things. After all, I pull off this act at work every day.

Tom tells me he's on his way to Zurich.

"I'm headed to London for ten days—but I love Zurich," I enthuse, with the savoir faire of the international traveler. "I was just there. You've been up the Jungfrau?"

"On the train? Of course! Hey, I'm making a stop in London on my way back. Give me the name of your hotel, Em. We've got a lot of catching-up to do." He winks with nostalgic innuendo at the woman he believes I still am.

I grab the napkin from under my cappuccino and write down the hotel information. The intimacy of college sweethearts wraps around us again. What might happen if we get together in London?

"My plane is boarding," he says, looking at his watch.

"Sorry—I don't want to make you late."

"No apologies, Emmy. It was great to see you! I'll call Thursday, when I get to London."

In the space left jarringly empty in me by his departure, a realization blossoms: Maybe this is a chance to make a new choice? Shoot for a different outcome?

Twenty minutes later, an attendant comes to tell me that my flight to Heathrow is boarding.

Amsterdam. Tokyo. Dubai.

I don't move. Then I dig around in my bag for my phone and call the car service.

When Balbir returns to pick me up, I'm waiting at the curb. I notice that he has placed a new, unopened box of Kleenex on the backseat. My eyes swamp with tears and I feel dizzy, suddenly. Disoriented.

That trip to Zurich. As I wandered from the train station at the top of the Jungfrau, snow was falling, blurring the view. I ducked under the loud yellow tape warning DANGER – ACHTUNG to get to the edge of the cliff, so tired of the person I'd become. Above all else, crushed by a weariness sleep could not remedy. Below, soft clouds muffled the precipitous drop. How comforting they looked, how restful. I wavered before the seduction of just falling forward into that welcoming, soft pillow of oblivion.

"Miss?" Balbir asks as the town car glides out onto the Belt Parkway. "Your destination, please?"

"Oh! Sorry. Home, please. West Eighty-first Street. I'm sorry to have called you back like this, but I've decided to go home. To my apartment." *Why do I always apologize?* "I guess this must seem really crazy, but I—"

"You forgot something," he states, and catches my eye in his rearview mirror.

Half an hour later, as the town car comes to a stop in front of my brownstone, I'm not sure what I'm doing. I have no plan. "Do you mind waiting? I'm so sorry to ask. If you're busy, I . . . don't want to hold you up."

"I will wait."

He opens my door and I emerge hesitantly, smiling at him to express my gratitude. The big grin that spreads across his face in return catches me off guard and infuses me with some bewildering blend of long-forgotten courage and new-sprung optimism in the face of conflict I have avoided for too long. This gruff, kind man who has no stake in my success makes me feel better about myself—more capable—than any of the slick investors I've made money for these past few years.

Balbir crosses his muscular arms in front of his chest and leans back against the town car. "Go on."

By the time I've climbed the two flights leading to the front door I'm fast-breathing with fear.

I'm doing this.

My keys jangle as I unlock the front door.

Reed is sitting on the floor, leaning back against the couch with his computer resting on his spread legs. "What are you doing back here?" he says, snapping the laptop shut—but not before I see a flash of skin. *Was he looking at porn?*

Men do this, of course. Some women, too. It's not really a betrayal, is it? I grasp at excuses.

"We need . . . to talk."

"You're right," he says, scrambling up from his awkward position on the rug beside the couch. "We do. For starters, you need to stop being such a fucking bitch to me."

I notice his bong squatting on the floor next to his laptop. Beside it sits a crumpled notecard, singed and blackened. From the soft pink and green on its unburnt corner, I recognize it as the woodblock print of cherry blossoms on creamy handmade paper I'd picked out during an assignment in Tokyo. I'd wanted to send him an offering, to tell him how much I loved and missed him. To say, after yet another blowup, that I wanted to make things right.

I can actually feel my heart breaking in this moment.

Reed follows my gaze. If he feels any remorse, it doesn't show. "What, Emily? My lighter's shot, so I had to use the stove-top burner and a scrap of paper. Don't get started with me—"

You forgot something, the driver had said.

Fucking right.

"GET OUT!" The ragged snarl that rips from my throat shocks us both; Reed shuffles back a step. "I want you to leave. Now. *NOW!*"

Over the careless destruction of this one, small notecard, I expand with fury beyond my own borders, with a force that is blinding and irreversible.

"I've had enough of your *shit*, Reed! You've never paid a dime of rent for this apartment. So, pack your things and get out!"

He recovers, draws himself up into attack mode. Starts to loom over me. But, somehow, I just expand and grow taller.

"Do you see that car down there?" I hiss, right into his face. "The driver is waiting for you. He'll drag you downstairs if you don't get out of here right now!" I have no idea if this is true.

Reed's confidence in his ability to intimidate me waivers and he turns away, and begins to smash around the apartment instead. Closet doors slam, hangers fly across the bedroom, books cascade onto the floor as he rifles through our bookshelf. He pants and huffs with angry drama, his long hair falling into his eyes as he stuffs clothes, his laptop, and his bong into his duffel bag.

"We're not finished!" he screams, but I catch a furtive look of calculation on his face as he glances out the window and down at the waiting car. The driver is bigger than he is. With one last "Fuck you, cunt!" my husband is gone.

I come down to earth as the fight instinct dissipates, regain my normal dimensions. Deflated, my body shakes uncontrollably and I look around me, blinking, as if to clear my vision.

The cozy brownstone apartment that I could just afford with my first job has become a dump, reeking of weed. It's painful to see things without the blinders of denial. A hole punched into the plaster of the living room wall makes me suck in my breath. I don't want to remember how close my face was to the angry fist that made it.

Amsterdam. Tokyo. Dubai.

Should I have just gotten on a plane to London as planned, or to one of those other places? Will the missed flight, the missed meeting with investors cost me my job? Without my job, who am I?

The rank smell of my own sweat unnerves me; I know I haven't heard the last of my husband.

Amsterdam. Tokyo. Dubai?

No.

In the cabinet above the kitchen sink sits my old stove-top espresso maker. I heat up some milk and make a better cappuccino than the one pulled from the fancy steam espresso machine in the airport executive lounge. The wreckage surrounds me. This next part is going to be hard.

I open the windows and let in the fresh air.

Thief

Summer began, and each day Anna followed the campus walkway past the lake and through immense flowering rhododendron bushes, entering by 8:45 a.m. into the silent and dimly lit sanctuary of the university's Rare Book Library. As a student summer employee, she dusted books or collected them in stacks to be treated in the Vacudyne machine for the prevention of mold.

June passed, and the weeks of July crept by. Anna became restless. As one day of diligent cleaning and cataloging blended into the next, loneliness and boredom weighed down on her. To her dismay, the row-upon-row, shelf-upon-shelf of mute, lifeless volumes hemmed her in and oppressed her. During the drawn-out afternoons, imagining other students with summer clerkships in busy offices or positions on boisterous teams engaged in field research deepened her despondency.

"I'm putting my trust in you, Anna, to hold down the fort for a few days," the head librarian informed her on a Thursday afternoon in early August. "I'll be out next week at the annual Rare Book Librarian's conference."

Anna sighed. "I don't imagine the books will misbehave in your absence."

"I dare say," responded the prim librarian.

The following Tuesday, alone in the hushed library and fending off an urge to doze, Anna began to catalog a newly donated collection of correspondence. Her eyes widened as she realized that the fragile notes were missives exchanged by two nineteenth-century English poets. Each letter was folded in upon itself to become its own envelope—so very small! With careful fingers she unfolded one and then the next. Each contained just a bare line or two.

They were love letters.

How surprised I was to learn of your visit, and how saddened to have been away and missed you!

Indeed! I had hoped to tell you in person what now I must pen in dry words—how much I admire your latest poem—and—you.

Please—won't you call again?

Anna began to read the letters aloud into the solemn quiet of the Rare Book Library:

"*Tell me when! And I will be at your door.*"

"*I beg thee, return,*" Anna whispered, "*whether it be day or night!*"

Anna held each precious artifact in her hands, amazed as the desire they conjured swept her through the afternoon and evening. Any one of the letters was small enough to fit into a pocket or handbag! And yet, every plaintive question, every breathless reply, seemed to kindle into a bonfire of passion. Her heart raced and her palms grew moist. Her imagination spun in a dizzy whirl of vicarious longing.

Anna no longer cared to be an intern in a busy office, nor a member of a team of field researchers. What she wanted had to do with these letters. How did one come to experience such extravagant feelings? What was it like to be the object of such devotion? Seated in the cool silence of antiquated books and letters, Anna woke up. She wanted more than anything else in the world *to know*.

To possess and be possessed.

Many years later, a student scrolled through the digitized collection of love letters.

Beloved Thief! Thou hast stolen my heart, abducted my soul! If I forsake all for thee—family, fortune, my good name—wilt thou come for me?

The student scratched her head. *But . . . what*, she wondered, *did he write to her, in reply?* There was no other letter.

Now a professor of English at the university, a middle-aged Anna expressed surprise. "One letter must be missing," she confirmed. "What a tantalizing literary mystery!"

Wilt thou come for me?

The long-dead letter writer and her lover would certainly have known the answer. And Anna knew it, too.

That evening, envisioning a path through rhododendrons to a quiet sanctuary of rare books and correspondence, Anna crossed her study to a bookcase and pulled down a college collection of poetry. Between two of its pages lay a faded sheet, folded in upon itself to form an envelope. Small enough to fit into a pocket or handbag.

Smoke

"Don't go."

Simon and Julia lay beside each other in bed, in a hotel in Kowloon. In the dark, the room seemed suspended in the night sky; the windows sweeping from floor to ceiling were an inconsequential barrier to the luminous harbor below. Across this waterway, resplendent for centuries with ships from every corner of the world, Hong Kong's Victoria Peak rose, glittering.

She hated this time, just before Simon left to go home to his wife. But she kept up the pretense that she could handle it—that it was better this way. Simon's clandestine attention wrapped around her like a velvet robe and made her feel singled out and desired. Her own brief marriage, before it had finally wrenched apart, had battered her self-confidence, leaving her bruised with loss. And Simon's marriage was obviously a sham, she had concluded, or why else would he be lying in bed with her?

They'd spent the evening at his club outside the city, swimming in the glowing night-lit pool, teasing each other underwater. Seated beside her at dinner, Simon had kissed her openly, passionately, while his hands had caressed her face and the curve of her neck, and slid down toward her breasts. She'd laughed with giddy, nervous pleasure at his indiscretion, while shrewd waiters looked away and other guests in the hushed and elegant dining room glanced at them, speculating.

Now, Simon rested on his elbow and smiled at her. With his finger, he traced the frown on her lips. Ignoring Julia's wistful entreaty to stay, he asked, "Did I ever tell you the story of how my grandmother committed murder?"

Simon Chao was the CEO and publisher of the Swan Prestige Magazine Group in Hong Kong, a privately held company run by the Chao family. Six months earlier Swan Prestige had hired Julia, a young, blond ex-pat recently moved from Chicago, to sell advertising space to other *gweilo*—white Westerners making the lucrative marketing decisions at American- and European-based companies in Hong Kong.

They had hit it off at once. Julia could tell that her relaxed, open manner attracted Simon and allowed him to step out from behind the wall of formality around being the boss. And she didn't hide her admiration for Simon's business acumen. Tall and athletic, with polished prep school English, Simon charmed female customers into seeing things his way. Difficult male customers he backed into a corner of inexorable defeat, using his understanding of their weaknesses to his advantage.

Simon invariably prevailed in negotiations, and without ever raising his voice. That subtle use of power excited Julia. She worked hard to impress her boss, and after four months of focused effort, she surpassed her sales target for the entire year.

Perhaps because she was an outsider—or maybe because, now that she had demonstrated her worth, he respected her as a professional—Simon began to confide in her. He complained about the burden of responsibility he felt to the family business.

His father still puttered around the office, holding the title of chairman of the board. "Don't let Dad fool you. He looks like a harmless old man, but he still disrespects me by challenging every single decision I make!"

Simon's vehemence surprised Julia. Actually, it made her feel sorry for him, despite his wealth and position.

One night, Simon and Julia were the last two to leave the office on Queen's Road, Central. She often worked late to avoid returning to her small flat, with its low ceilings, miserly windows, and the unfamiliar cooking smells coming from next door.

Standing beside each other in the steel-and-mirrored elevator, Simon turned to Julia, his expression intense and questioning. "I wish I could be like you, Julia—*free*!" Then, to her astonishment, he kissed her. "You're like sunshine, Julia!" he exclaimed. "You're like fresh air to me in this stale, tiresome place!" Her better judgment deserted her, and she gave in, unresisting, to his embrace.

In their five-star hotel room, Simon eased back against the pillows. "It was in the 1920s," he continued. She curled toward him beneath the silken sheets as if everything were okay, and rested her head on his shoulder.

But everything was not okay. Simon was speaking to her as if she were a child—as if he were telling her a bedtime story before he tucked her in and left her. It was becoming harder for Julia to ignore as the weeks, then months, went by, the growing awareness that being with Simon hurt more than it felt good.

"My grandparents were taking a rare holiday at the beach, with the children," he said. "At some point my grandmother got up to use the toilet. Suddenly, my grandfather heard screams. He ran to see what was happening and came upon my grandmother being attacked by a young thug.

"My grandfather fought the attacker but the guy had a knife and, in the struggle, my grandfather was stabbed and killed. My grandmother cried for help and a group of villagers rushed to the scene, drawn by all the commotion.

"In the middle of that chaos, the thug took off—but the villagers chased after him. Eventually, they caught up with him and drove him up into a tree. They circled around so there was no way he could escape.

"The villagers kept that young man trapped up in the tree until my grandmother arrived, screaming hysterically and smeared with my grandfather's blood.

"'What should we do with him?' they shouted to her. 'Should we kill him, or let him go?'

"'Burn him!' she howled.

"So, the villagers piled dry grass and straw around the tree as the man begged and screamed for mercy. They ignored his pleas, set the grass on fire, and burned him to death. My grandmother and the villagers stood vigil until there was nothing left but the skeleton of a tree, wreathed in choking gray smoke that filled their eyes and mouths and clung to their clothes."

Simon regarded her coolly.

"Why are you telling me this?" She sat up in bed now, stiff and straight. The gruesome, tragic story had made her feel nauseous. This was not how she had expected their romantic evening to end.

Without responding to her question, Simon rose to dress. He moved through the room as gracefully as a cat, his body smooth and golden. It was nearly two o'clock in the morning—why did he even bother going home?

Anger flared in Julia, and she shocked both herself and Simon by bursting out, "I admire your grandmother! She loved your grandfather so passionately that she let those villagers set his killer on fire!" *How unlike you, Simon!* Julia wanted him to hear. *You're too cowardly to do anything more than go home to your frigid marriage!*

"Yes, my grandmother acted out of passion," Simon said quietly, sitting on a low ottoman opposite the bed and slipping on his Gucci loafers. "And she regretted that decision as long as she lived. After all, my grandfather was dead. But now, until her dying day, she would hear that young man screaming in agony as he was burned alive."

He paused. Then he stared at her across the tousled bed covers. "Too much passion"—he spoke each word with care—"only leads to regret."

In the morning, at work, Julia did a double-take as she passed Simon's office. His face, she saw, was streaked with red scratches.

She overheard him explain to his assistant that his wife's temperamental bichon frise had lashed out as he'd tried to cuddle the little dog.

But later, when Simon asked Julia to come into his office, under the pretense of reviewing an advertising deal, he ended the conversation by touching the inflamed claw marks on his cheek. "My wife," he said in a low voice, "has begun to object to my evening activities."

Simon's wife had appeared on several occasions, sweeping imperiously into the office in elaborate designer outfits, a Prada bag slung across her arm. She was as beautiful as a model, Julia had to admit, yet radiated dissatisfaction and resentment. *This woman is the cause of Simon's unhappiness*, she had assumed.

The possibility that it might have been the other way around never occurred to her.

"We live separate lives," Simon began, "but . . ." He let the statement hang, as if she would, of course, come to the appropriate conclusion.

In a flash she understood: Simon was dumping her. Of course—that had been the point of his story in the early hours of the morning. How naive she had been! Stupid. Tears filled her eyes before she could turn away from him.

"Why don't you come with us, Jules? Get out of the office and have some fun for a change." Ewan from the magazine's design department was inviting her to join him and some of his office mates for drinks. His crooked smile and tough-guy skinhead appearance disguised the fact that Ewan was bashful and kind, a man who would go out of his way to show you how to get to the subway after your first day at work. Which was how she and Ewan had first met.

Now at the noisy, beer-drenched karaoke bar in Lan Kwai Fong, Julia sank back into the booth, surrounded by Ewan's hodgepodge of friends. She settled into a warm, comfortable beer buzz, and into the unexpected relief of having nothing to prove.

Several pints in, Ewan got up to sing—shout—"I Can't Get No Satisfaction!" on the karaoke stage. Sloshed, but not to be outdone by Ewan's boldness, Julia marched to the front of the bar and responded by taking a stand for American schmaltz with an off-key rendition of "You Light Up My Life." Julia's new gang of friends—Chinese coworkers and ex-pat misfits like herself—clapped and whistled appreciatively above the noise of the crowded room.

At the end of the evening Julia and Ewan staggered out of the bar, arm in arm, drunk and laughing uproariously at each other's stupid jokes.

After that night, Julia no longer lingered around the Swan Prestige offices in case Simon happened to be working late and happened to change his mind and decide they could sneak out together for a few hours. In fact, sometimes she left early now, with Ewan. Then she'd find out the next day, from Simon's assistant, that her boss had come round looking for her.

The knowledge that Simon had sought her out unsuccessfully gave Julia some small, retaliatory satisfaction. She didn't worry about her job security. After all, she had just landed another big account—a lucrative three-year contract with Fresh Face Cosmetics—thanks to a fortuitous run-in at the karaoke bar.

On a Saturday morning as Julia finished her sales report for the week, Ewan turned up outside her cubicle holding a small plate with a fat slice of cake on it. "It's someone's birthday in our department, so . . ." He set down the plate with the creamy, sugary confection on her desk, accompanied by a plastic fork.

Simon appeared beside them, squash racket resting on his shoulder, clearly on his way out for the weekend. Before Julia had a chance to introduce the two men, Simon confronted Ewan. "Are you one of our employees?"

"Yes, sir. In Graphic Design."

Simon's cold glance slid from Ewan to Julia and back again, and just before turning away in the direction of the elevators, he remarked—with unmistakable sarcasm—"Are we paying our workers now to distribute cake?"

Julia watched as Simon strolled off, swinging the racket. Why? Why was it still so painful to see him walk away from her?

"A real wanker, the boss," Ewan remarked cheerfully as he helped himself to a big, messy forkful of her cake. "You should try some of this."

Simon called Julia at home that evening.

"Simon? Is everything okay?" He had never done this before, calling her at her flat. But then, why would he have, when previously she had always made herself so easily available at work?

"Congratulations on winning the Fresh Face account. I'm very pleased with you. I also wanted to say that I . . . miss our conversations. Don't you, Julia? I made a dinner reservation for us at the club tonight. To celebrate. With a bottle of Cristal."

The hot intensity of Simon's voice, and the assumption that she would acquiesce to his desire, nearly cornered Julia into saying yes. She hesitated. The vision of Simon leading her to a table at his club that he had selected especially for the two of them beckoned. How good it would feel to have Simon's hand pressed against the small of her back, even if that seductive gesture only created the illusion that she had a place in his world.

The threads of a life that belonged to *her*, a life that Julia was just beginning to weave together, tugged at her. And for reasons she would puzzle over later—spite? Self-preservation? The uncomplicated pleasure of an evening alone in her tiny flat that finally felt like home?—she said, "I can't, Simon. I'm busy tonight, but . . . hello? Simon?"

Silence blistered on the other end of the line for several long seconds before Julia heard the abrupt, empty buzz of a dial tone.

"Leave the door open," Simon instructed when he called Julia into his office on Monday morning. Before she could even sit, he informed her that she was being fired.

Julia froze, dumbfounded by his impassive expression. *How dare he!* She knew that she was good at her job. She had made his company a lot of money. He had to consider that, didn't he? Without taking her eyes from his face, she reached back and shoved the glass door shut, in defiance of his orders.

"Is this to punish me," she demanded, "because I wouldn't have dinner with you on Saturday?" She was beyond caring whether others could hear her—whether she—or he—might lose face. Simon glared at her without speaking, his features ignited with anger. He scoffed. "Don't flatter yourself." The two stared at each other for a long time, until Julia, cheeks burning, had to concede. She looked away and out the window, toward the harbor. "*Why,* then?" Her voice wavered.

Had Julia believed she could strike a business deal with love? Offering just a part-time, after-hours exposure of her heart, that would somehow leave her less vulnerable to hurt and loneliness? That she could sidestep the unpredictability of Simon's emotions and demands, his own conflicted longings?

As Simon got up and came out from behind the expanse of his desk, Julia noticed a framed photograph of his grandmother—both murderer and denouncer of passion—sitting on the table behind his chair. So: Grandmother was watching him.

"You're not going to answer me?" She found herself challenging him now, as she glanced from the photo of his grandmother back to Simon. Once he had told her he wanted to be free. Why couldn't he just admit that in the end, for him, there was too much to lose? Family and business, the glamour and safety of his ivory tower life.

Simon walked toward her. The heat of his body reached her, though he stopped short as if in reproach—as if there might have been some way that Julia could have prevented both Simon's desire for her and its unfortunate outcome.

Hands resting inside the pockets of his linen trousers, Simon kept his distance as he and Julia stood facing each other. The silence, thick and heavy, encircled them like smoke.

There was nothing Julia wanted to take with her, so she rode the elevator down to the lobby empty-handed. Out in Hong Kong harbor, red-sailed Chinese junks crisscrossed the water among the huge container ships; the Star ferry chugged purposefully toward Kowloon and splendid, stately yachts cruised to beaches and the outer islands, each vessel setting its own course. Julia strode across the vast marble reception gallery. The magisterial sliding glass doors parted for her as she stepped outside to face the raucous, liberating clamor of the city.

I Found You

Meg's phone jangled to life and she turned from her office window with its view of the snow-covered village.

"Hello? My name is Jade. I'm looking for . . . Megan Evans?"

"This is Meg."

The young caller hesitated. "Oh, um . . . Meg? I'm wondering . . ." And then the words tumbled out. "I'm wondering if there's a person whose call you've been waiting for?"

Meg worked as a business consultant, and callers who didn't get straight to the point annoyed her. She felt tempted to hang up on this *Jade*, probably some rookie telemarketer. Instead, she responded tersely to the question: "I'm sorry—*what?*"

"Is Megan Evans the name you had in high school?" the girl pressed on.

"It is."

"Did you graduate from Scarsdale High School, in New York, sometime between 1992 and 1996?"

"Yes, I did." Meg found herself softening. "But . . . what is this about?"

Jade's voice quavered. "Is there . . . *someone you've missed?*"

Meg stayed silent. It was as if the answer to a crossword had suddenly appeared before her eyes, the word dropping into the empty puzzle boxes. She thought she understood what Jade might be hinting at.

Alone in the office she shared with her longtime boyfriend, Robbie, Meg stared at the falling snow that blurred her view of the outside world. Robbie was scheduled to be at a job site, one of the crew for a house renovation. But at four o'clock on a cold February afternoon, Meg had little expectation that he was still at work; Robbie had probably settled in with the boys at the brewery around the corner.

Not for the first time, Meg stifled her dissatisfaction and disappointment. She resisted wading too deep into the muck of self-reflection and considered instead the alternatives before her. Would it be so wrong to follow where this curious phone call led?

When Jade, without further explanation, requested a meeting, Meg—without further questions—agreed.

"You look just like your yearbook picture!" Jade exclaimed after they'd exchanged an awkward half-embrace. The waitress showed them to their table at the café overlooking the Grand Central Station concourse. The commuter train station happened to be a convenient meeting place for them both.

"I mean it! You still look like me at eighteen." Jade leaned across the small table and stared at Meg. "That picture was how I knew! I knew you were my mother!"

Mother. Meg let the word sink in.

Though piercings in her eyebrow toughened Jade's pretty, elfin face, the younger woman had a point: the two of them shared the same striking blue eyes tilting up at the corners, the dark brown hair, a rather sharp chin. Meg calculated that Jade must be twenty-seven or twenty-eight.

"The adoption agency could only tell me that my birth mother had grown up in Scarsdale, New York. So I went to the local library, found all the yearbooks from the years that might be possible. I searched for a match, for a girl who looked like me. And I found you! Megan Evans! I'm so excited to meet you—at last."

Jade laughed and chattered, giddy and triumphant, as they drank their coffees. Meg barely said a word. She imagined herself through Jade's eyes: the fulfillment of so much longing and hope. An overwhelming desire to be that person for this exuberant young woman swelled up in her chest, stifling all sense of right and wrong. Even worse, Meg found herself nodding and smiling encouragingly.

When at last they parted, after many hugs, they agreed to speak again soon.

The next day, back at their office, Meg found Robbie's Amex bill, which he had pointedly left on her desk. "I thought we'd agreed you would cover your own charges for your business," she reminded him. His card was linked to her account.

"It's just for another month. I'm expecting payment on some big invoices any day."

"That's what you've been saying for months. You've got to pay these or get your own separate account, Robbie. I mean it."

"Really, Meg? I've got news for you. I'm your partner, not your kid. Maybe you want to stop acting like my *mother*."

Given the twelve years between them, the barb hit its target.

Their age difference hadn't seemed important when he was in his twenties and she in her thirties. On the contrary, it had struck them both as unconventional, sexy. Then Meg's forty-fifth birthday had come and gone, as had her desire for marriage and hope for the family she'd once imagined.

They'd retreated into their own, separate social circles. Spending time with Robbie and his friends now made it depressingly clear how young they all were, how little in common she had with them. With bleak clarity, she thought of the snowmobile, the new Jeep, and the fishing boat she'd purchased at Robbie's urging—what were these, if not grown-up toys?

Jade rang a week after their meeting, eager to connect again.

Meg had thought about what she'd say when this inevitable call came. She took a deep breath, paused . . . and then confessed. "When I heard your voice on the phone that first time . . . heard what you had to say . . . I don't know what came over me, Jade. I wanted to meet you. And then . . . I so wished your theory had been correct. But the truth is, I've never been pregnant. I'm sorry. I hope your mother is out there somewhere but I'm not the one you're looking for."

"What?" said Jade, her voice pitched high. "But you— How could you! Why didn't you tell me right away?"

"Jade, I'm so—"

But Jade had already hung up on her.

Because, Meg thought as she closed her eyes, flushed with shame, *I let myself indulge in the fantasy of a different choice I might have made. Because I was only thinking of myself. Because I was trying for a redo of my life.*

It was in that instant that the resolve to end things with Robbie solidified in her mind. He'd hit the nail on the head, hadn't he? She'd been acting like his mother. Somehow, they'd both stood by and let this happen.

But that was a person she'd never intended to be.

The following spring, as she gazed out at the daffodils coming into bloom outside her office, Meg received a surprise call from Jade.

"I tracked her down, Meg. My *real* birth mother."

Meg felt her heart contract. She said, "That's wonderful news, Jade! I'm so glad you called."

"I—I just figured—"

"I wouldn't have blamed you if you never wanted to speak to me again. What I did was . . . well, it was unforgiveable."

"Yeah, I was pretty pissed," Jade agreed. "And I still don't get why you would do that. Get my hopes up. But the thing is . . . I felt a connection with you. When I found your picture in the yearbook, and then met you in person, I *wanted* you to be my mother." Jade's voice broke. "So . . . I was really disappointed. But after a while, I figured, whatever, and I started looking again."

"I . . . I see."

"The woman I found—my *mother*—she wasn't at all what I expected. I think she felt the same way about me. We had a couple of visits but, I don't know. I doubt we'll see each other again. Anyway, I wanted you to know . . . and also, that I've decided to forgive you."

The silence stretched out between them, as each woman grappled with her own disappointed dreams. Then Jade spoke up first. "We both like cappuccino, right?" she asked, hesitant—and hopeful.

"Yes," Meg ventured.

"What would you think about meeting up again sometime? You know . . . you and me?"

Was it Meg's imagination, or had Jade's voice suddenly become light, like an April breeze beckoning with possibility.

"Only this time we just try to be . . . *friends*."

The Swimming Pool

The dog and I swim through the soft turquoise depths, in languid loopy circles. He nudges his yellow ball, feet paddling beneath him. I hold my plastic margarita goblet from a set of twelve you and I bought, imagining pool parties. It tips above the water in my unsteady grasp, though now there's no one to care if it drops or spills.

Sometimes I hear the train whistle: the long line of cars pulls in, and then heads on to someplace better. Sometimes I drink too much, my head full of angry conversations where this time I come out the winner. Tonight, I float on my back as another day expires and the

world becomes dark. But if I keep looking up, I see that the stars are moving, ever so slowly.

You and I conjured our shared dream of paradise, planting lush hibiscus trees along the pebbly border. Now the blood-red blossoms unfurl, dropping gently into the water as all is lost. Tomorrow the movers will come to take away your boxes of things, your furniture.

But I will still have this swimming pool. Don't you remember? Once, we bought this house for the pool.

The Shower Room

A hundred women before her had probably worn the thick, spongy loaner bathing suit. *At least.* And today, showing up for class in this lumpy relic had nearly overwhelmed Marie with the feeling that she somehow stuck out as hopelessly dorky and pathetic. She couldn't wait to take a shower and get her clothes on again. Who in the world would arrive to a swim class without her own suit? What had she been thinking?

When Marie had stumbled out of her freshman dorm room at the college, half asleep at 7:45 a.m., heading to Beginning French, she'd actually not been thinking about swim class at all. Earlier that morning, the sound of groaning had awakened her as she lay in the dark, in the tiny unfamiliar room. She'd tried to orient herself to the tight space jammed with two beds, dressers, desks, and bookshelves. In the opposite bed, a mound of covers had heaved as somewhere beneath it a creature—her roommate, Fiona—tossed and turned.

Perilously close to sliding into the pit of homesickness, Marie had thrown off her quilt, pulled on sweatpants and a T-shirt, and

gone down to breakfast. She'd secretly feared that whatever unhappiness Fiona's mournful sighs expressed might suck her in, too.
When she'd gone back up to get ready for class, the lump in the
opposite bed was gone.

All morning, Marie had been thinking about taking a nap. She'd
forgotten about Introductory Lap Swim, so she had ended up being
unprepared and looking foolish. Now, class over, she heaved herself up out of the frigid water and onto the pool edge, her baggy
one-piece catching and pulling against the concrete. The suit had
been borrowed at the gym check-in. She needed a bathing suit of
her own, but that would require walking into town to buy one.

She shuffled across the pool area toward the lockers, a thin
white towel partially hiding the ill-fitting garment. Her eyes were
stinging from the chlorine and her mass of dark, curly hair felt as
stiff as hay. She really needed that shower.

A steamy warmth enveloped her in the shower room, a space
that was pleasingly simple and unadorned. This was a women's
college, so there was only one shower room—for women. Marie's
shoulders relaxed after being hunched up around her neck. She and
the eight other students had just spent the past hour swimming laps
and then standing around in the freezing-cold pool, listening to
their instructor.

The stalls near the shower room entrance were missing shower
curtains. Marie scanned the entire room for a stall she could use and
realized that no curtains hung in front of any of the stalls. How had
she not noticed this on her way to the pool at the beginning of class?

Another girl, a freshman like her but wearing her own
sleek, black bathing suit, followed her in. Marie recognized the

girl—Cecilia—from her dorm. Then three more girls joined them. They all looked at the open stalls and then at one another.

Cecilia muttered out loud what they all were asking themselves: "How do they think we're supposed to take showers?"

Uncertain—and therefore annoyed—the girls filed through to the dressing room and the individual lockers where each had stored her clothes. No one showered. Each girl found a corner of the dressing room and turned her back to the others.

Marie peeled off the bathing suit, her body hunched, then shoved her legs and arms into her baggy green army pants, sweatshirt, jean jacket. She buckled on her flat-heeled ankle boots.

Intentionally, if somewhat self-consciously, she had started dressing in a way that was meant to show the world who she wanted to be: an artist. Or, at least some kind of rebellious person who rejected the tight-fitting clothes women were supposed to wear specifically to appeal to men. But with her dark hair wild and strawlike, she was pretty sure she looked more like a witch or a crazy person than a free-spirited bohemian.

Alone, she returned her wet suit and exited the gym.

Three days later, Marie was back at the pool, mentally prepared this time for the dowdy loaner bathing suit. Classes, homework, freshman meetings, and getting lost while following the meandering campus pathways had left her no extra time to purchase a suit of her own. On top of all those excuses, the prospect of viewing her reflection in a dressing-room mirror—pale flesh jammed into a thin, revealing nylon swimsuit—had not exactly put her in the mood to shop.

It had never occurred to her to pack a suit in her college trunk. But then, during the week of orientation before classes began, she'd scanned the options for mandatory freshman Phys Ed. Introductory Lap Swim seemed the only choice that didn't involve hitting things or smashing into anyone. Team sports were out. Marie's high school exposure to the win-or-lose ferocity of contact sports had convinced her for all time that she was not a team player.

She could, on the other hand, imagine herself swimming, facedown in the long, blue lap lane, in water as cold and quiet as outer space. Weightlessly cutting through the liquid silence, she could lose herself in her thoughts, uninterrupted by someone in cleats trying to run her down and kill her with a field hockey stick or conk her on the head with a volleyball.

Now as she walked through the shower room toward the pool, she averted her gaze from the figure who stood in one of the curtainless stalls, naked under a hot shower. The girl was just standing there, showering. Completely exposed! Though she'd barely glanced at her, Marie was almost certain the girl was Cecilia.

Tall, and with the erect posture of a dancer, or a police sergeant, Cecilia came across as very sure of herself. With envy, Marie had observed her dashing off assignments during lunch for the philosophy course they shared—literally a minute before class. The professor had returned Cecilia's first assignment with a big A+ scrawled across the top in red, while Marie, who had labored over hers, had earned only a B. Cecilia also had her own car, a sign to Marie of her greater, adult-like independence.

And now, Cecilia had evidently conquered the initial shyness that all the girls had shared. She nonchalantly showered with no curtain around her for privacy.

Marie walked out to the pool, sat down on the edge, and tested the cold water with her feet. The instructor had outlined her expectations during their first class, striding around the pool with long, tanned legs that suggested days filled with nothing *but* swimming laps, in an outdoor pool, say, in sunny Florida. Not one inside a chilly gym in Massachusetts. Seventy-two laps—*more than a mile!*—three times a week, she'd announced, with a goal of completing the laps in under forty-five minutes.

Marie had scowled and her teeth had chattered. She had to be kidding, right?

Weekly laps could be accomplished under the honor code, the instructor had continued, meaning that students could swim on their own, any time during the week, and keep track of their results. But she did not, apparently, trust her students' "honor" entirely: They would have to clock in and out at the front desk of the gym, and the instructor would be checking the time sheets.

The instructor had not been kidding.

How was Marie going to do this?

Today, she had to admit she liked it here, in the big, open, blue-gray-white space. The enormity of it, the absence of people talking. It reminded her of a museum or a church—which was weird because the pool was obviously not at all like the Catholic church her family attended.

Even the smell of chlorine in the warm, humid air soothed her. Strange. The view of trees outside the bank of high windows caught her eye, too. Fall leaves changing to gold and scarlet fluttered and drifted in the air, carried by a breeze. It was so . . . unhurried. Gentle. She eased off the rough ledge and began swimming back and forth across the twenty-five-meter pool.

One, two. Three, four.

How was it, Marie brooded, that this other girl—Cecilia— could just stand there, stark naked, in the open shower room? She felt defensive and critical—it was not something *she* would ever do. From her brief, embarrassed glance, she had observed that Cecilia was neither thin nor fat. It wasn't like she had some amazing body to show off, like she was a model or anything. She was just . . . herself. Naked. Taking a shower.

The word DANGER in big, neon-red capital letters lit up inside Marie's brain. Didn't Cecilia feel awfully . . . vulnerable?

Marie was too fat. "Thunder Thighs," a group of unkind girls in high school had nicknamed her. No way had their family doctor been right when he'd informed her that, to the contrary, her weight fell in the "average" range for her age and height. Despite her haphazard attempts to get into a routine of sit-ups, her belly felt soft. She hated how embarrassing her nipples looked to her— too big. And her breasts didn't stand up the way she assumed they were supposed to, but hung softly on her chest. Her body looked and felt all wrong.

Lap thirteen, fourteen.

She would never even consider saying out loud that she didn't like her body. That would sound prudish and antifeminist. But now, in the safe embrace of the pool, swimming back and forth, something inside Marie relaxed. She breathed deeply, evenly, one stroke after the next stroke after the next. It felt okay to admit to herself that her body made her uncertain. Scared. Sometimes it seemed like a thing apart, a thing she had a hard time owning. Her eyes stung with underwater tears. If she were honest, sometimes her body felt like an alien being she was at war with.

Twenty-five, twenty-six.

She kicked off hard from the pool's edge and propelled herself into her next lap with an unexpected surge of anger. Too many other people seemed to think they had some claim to her body!

Her mother had regularly worked herself into near hysterics ever since Marie had gotten her first period, at twelve. Before that, Marie had moved about her child's world freely, like a wild animal. Girls and boys had all run around together playing in the neighborhood. Then suddenly, Marie's body had turned into a ticking time bomb! Those same boys, or so her mother insisted, "just wanted one thing." They were intent on detonating her like an explosive!

Marie had resented that she had to be on guard now, in a way her brothers did not. By ten o'clock at night her parents expected her to be home, while her brothers had no curfew. The boys lived as they always had, while she had become a prisoner of war under her parents' constant surveillance, threatened with getting thrown out of the house should she allow her body to misbehave in some reckless way.

Marie gasped for breath. Why couldn't her parents see that their fear and lack of trust in her had just made her angry and confused—and uncertain if *she* could trust *herself*?

Forty-seven, forty-eight.

That was it. Forty-eight laps were all Marie could swim today.

She grasped the side of the pool, puffing, trying to catch her breath. Her instructor with the long Florida legs strolled into the pool area and straight over to Marie. She leaned down to talk.

"It's Marie, right? You've got a good, strong kick, Marie!"

Marie had not expected the praise. She smiled like a goofy little kid.

"When you take a stroke, try not to lift your head up out of the water. Think about making a rotating motion with your chest, from left to right, and just allow your head to turn naturally for a breath with each stroke. And don't forget: Raise each arm up from the elbow."

Marie nearly swaggered into the shower room. She hadn't thought that anything about the way she lumbered through the water was right, but her instructor's comment that she had "a good, strong kick" had given her a burst of self-confidence. Her thighs weren't "big" or "fat"; they were *strong*.

She stood tall, enjoying the thick steam cocooning her. She ran her fingers up one of the smooth, light-brown tiled walls. She pressed her feet down and spread her toes against the warm tile floor. The warmth felt like acceptance. Should she take a shower?

But . . . like hypervigilant parents, her feet began moving her past the showers to the secluded safety of the farthest corner of the locker room.

On Friday afternoon, Marie set off from campus and walked into town. In a sporting goods store, a Speedo suit with a purple tie-dye design fit perfectly. On Saturday, clutching her new suit, swim cap, and goggles—and with the instructor's suggestions in mind—she returned to the pool.

She'd approach the class like a real swimmer. She dove in.

Lap one, two.

Churning through the vast, silent blue of the pool, her mind slipped back to her junior year in high school. Her boyfriend, Jordan, then a senior, had been obsessed with having sex. He'd badgered her endlessly with "When are we going to do it?" and they'd spent hours making out in his car. Jordan would try to get his hands between her legs, while Marie, aroused and horny, the crotch of her jeans wet, would burn with frustration at her body's unruly desires—and at her boyfriend for pushing and trying to direct everything. He never gave her a chance to figure out what she wanted.

They'd end up exhausted, disappointed, and angry at each other. She'd be relieved to get away from him and back to the safety of her house. Why was it that her body, too, seemed to have its own agenda, and was at war with her mind?

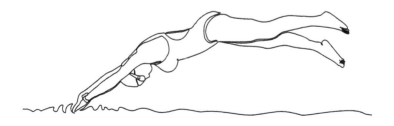

Nineteen, twenty.

Marie realized she felt more at ease in the water now, like she had a right to be here. Rolling from side to side, turning her head from right to left, lifting her arms from the elbows, it all worked! With her improved form, Marie's confident strokes pulled her through the water as fast as the girl in the adjacent lane. Faster, even.

Thirty-three, thirty-four.

It pissed her off that she was supposed to listen to, and take into account, everyone else's opinions about how her body looked, and what she should and shouldn't do with it. In the end, the only strategy Marie had been able to come up with to fend off her parents' oppressive fear and control—as well as the unfair and untrue accusation by Jordan that she was a "cock tease"—had been to separate herself from the object of everyone's relentless fixation. To make an enemy of her own body.

Fifty-five, fifty-six.

She wished she wasn't divided into so many pieces. There was her brain that seemed to be on constant high alert, especially in this new place. And then there was her unpredictable body, driven by its own impulses.

Sixty-seven, sixty-eight.

Who was she, and who did she want to become? These questions came from her heart—the most hidden and unknown of all the pieces. She didn't want to be broken like this, cutting herself on her own sharp edges. She wanted to be one smooth, whole person.

Seventy-one . . . Seventy-two!

Marie stood at the shallow end of the pool, breathless, smiling. She'd done it! Seventy-two laps! Over a mile! Okay, she'd been swimming for more than an hour, but so what? She'd done it.

In the shower room, Marie saw two girls, each in her own curtainless stall, standing naked under the hot water. Soaping up, washing their hair. Marie stood still in the warm safety of the tiled space, trying not to look at them. Trying to name the feelings that rose up inside and threatened to choke her. Ultimately, she landed on: *ashamed* and *afraid*. How did those girls feel comfortable enough to expose themselves like that?

Were they that different from her?

Earlier that day, on her way across campus, Marie had heard an unbelievably awful noise that turned out to be her roommate, Fiona, playing bagpipes on the green. Fiona had blushed bright red when Marie walked up to her. "It's pretty loud, right?" she'd admitted, abashed and apologetic.

"No! I mean, well *yes*, it's pretty loud," Marie had said, "but . . . it's so *different*, too. I think it's cool that you play bagpipes."

Later, in the cafeteria, she'd found an empty chair at the lunch table where Cecilia sat. Marie made up her mind to join her intimidating dormmate. As they'd talked, she learned how hard Cecilia worked to live up to the expectations of her famous parents, both actors on TV. "You're so confident, Marie," Cecilia had sighed. "Like, how you dress—just the way you please. You never act as if you're trying to impress anyone."

Marie had not considered that her baggy wardrobe—partly a statement, but also, she had to admit, partly a disguise—might come across to anyone as a sign of self-confidence. To say the least.

Maybe all the girls felt nervous and insecure, in one way or another.

Now, in the shower room, despite the triumph of her seventy-two laps, she hesitated. Then, she walked with determination into a curtainless stall. Still wearing her bathing suit, she turned on the hot water and felt the muscles of her body relax under the pounding heat. But this was stupid, showering with clothes on. Was anyone really looking at her? Passing judgment on her? And if they were, did it matter to her now, the way it might have when Marie was younger and surrounded by the cliques and popularity contests of high school?

Last spring, right before the end of high school, that younger version of Marie told her parents she was staying with a girlfriend but instead took a bus to visit Jordan for a long weekend at his college.

A smiling young woman named Debbie popped into the common room Jordan shared with his two college roommates, offering a plate of freshly baked chocolate-chip cookies. As she assessed Debbie's tight T-shirt and short shorts, Marie tried to hide her jealousy and instantaneous dislike. Debbie even asked if the young men had *any laundry* they wanted to add to the load she was just about to do!

Debbie was so pretty, and yet Marie could see her straining for their approval. Did trying to win guys' affection, she wondered, automatically make girls feel like they had to act like their mothers— or their maids?

That weekend, however, Marie had something more important on her mind than Debbie and her cookies: sex. Specifically, whether she and Jordan were finally going to "do it." As she neared graduation, Marie was determined to lose her virginity. A Catholic school virgin! What a childish cliché. There was no way she was arriving at college without having had sex at least once.

Saturday night while Jordan's roommates were out partying, she and Jordan remained back in the dorm suite, alone.

"Do you have condoms? Because I snuck a few, from my brother. In case." In her nervousness at being squeezed beside Jordan, both of them naked in his single bed, Marie shivered under the thin bed sheet and tried to sound assertive. Prepared.

"I *know* what I'm doing, Marie," he said dismissively. He reached for his wallet, which lay on the night table, and pulled out a foil square. He bit the corner to tear it open and fumbled with the slippery rubber tubing. He climbed on top of her and then . . . she gasped from the sharp jab. A few struggling thrusts later, it was all over.

Was that it? Was that what all the threats and arguments and drama had been about?

"For future reference? Try not to direct everything . . . it's kind of a turnoff," Jordan grumbled before turning his back on her. "I don't care what all the 'feminists' say." He fell asleep, leaving Marie to feel irredeemably unattractive—and sad. So, this is what it was like, then, between grown-up women and men.

On Sunday morning, she overheard Jordan laughing with other guys in the common room. "Oh, Jesus! That's so sick!" one of them snorted. Something about their tone—like the high-pitched, squeamish laughter of little boys torturing some small animal—summoned a sense of dread inside Marie.

When Jordan returned to the bedroom where she was getting dressed, Marie asked, "What? What were you all laughing about out there?"

Jordan looked embarrassed. Like he didn't want to say. *"What?"*

"About Debbie, if it's so important for you to know. There was a party at Sigma Chi. People are saying she drank too much, got wasted . . ." Jordan turned all serious and distant. "Then I guess she disappeared into one of the frat bedrooms. Let a bunch of guys have sex with her."

"'Disappeared into a bedroom?' 'Let a bunch of guys have sex with her'? *That sounds like rape*, Jordan. Like your friends raped the cookie girl, who does your laundry for you!" Stiff with shock, Marie sat down on the rumpled bed sheet, on the verge of being sick.

She couldn't help imagining pretty Debbie's injured, used body. A body that was, after all, like hers. Maybe Debbie had believed she and the guys at the party were all buddies. But in the end, she'd been nothing more to them than that empty plate of cookies. Here, they might as well have said, you can take this now. We're finished.

"Where's Debbie now?" Marie asked. "Did anyone check to see if she's okay?"

"How should I know? I doubt she'll ever want to show her face in class again, though."

"*Are you serious, Jordan?* It's your friends who should be ashamed. They should be kicked out of school! She should report those guys to the campus police."

"Keep it down, okay, Marie? Jesus Christ . . . *it was a party*."

As she began to throw things into her suitcase, her ears were ringing. She wanted to block Jordan out as he made more excuses for his friends' behavior. On what planet was it okay for Jordan to pretend it was perfectly normal for multiple guys to have sex with one drunk girl because *it was a party?*

Jordan rolled his eyes and spoke to her in his new, worldly college voice. The voice that came from a person she no longer knew. "Don't be so naive, Marie."

She stared at him, until he looked down at his feet.

"Should I walk you to the bus stop?" he asked, as though he already knew the answer.

"Don't bother."

Lugging her suitcase, Marie marched past his surprised roommates and out the door as messy tears streamed down her face.

In the shower room, Marie peeled off her bathing suit and hung it over the tile dividing wall. The sense of vulnerability she felt was excruciating, her embarrassment dreadful.

DANGER!

She glanced across the room. One of the girls had gone and the other one was paying no attention to her. She took a deep breath, felt the warm water pounding on her, thrumming all over her body and calming her down. Smoothing her sharp edges.

In her *real life*, the one that started now, she could wash her parents' fears and demands and the immature pettiness of high school right off herself, watch all of it slip through her fingers, swirl between her toes, disappear down the drain.

In her new, real life, she would not allow her *ex*-boyfriend Jordan's callous view of the world to stifle or intimidate her. Down the drain with that, too! Let him try to feel better about himself by calling her naive. That just made him a coward.

The truth was, she'd decided to expect something more—something better—between herself and men, even if she couldn't yet imagine what that might be.

She lifted her hair and let the water rinse through it. She ran her hands down herself and felt a sense of tenderness for her soft breasts, her strong thighs. Silently, she apologized to her body for considering it too fat, or somehow wrong. Or dangerous or untrustworthy. Her body was her ally, not her enemy.

Marie was strong, after all. She had a body that could swim seventy-two laps! A body that held her heart and mind and belonged to her.

More girls came in. More taps turned on. Steam billowed all around them. Then one by one, the young women finished washing up, swiveled their taps to *Off*, wrapped their hair in towels. They walked around the shower room as if they were strolling across campus, at once unguarded and unassailable.

In this place—here, now—they were no longer obsessed with nakedness or frightened by their own vulnerabilities. Standing among the other women as she toweled her body dry, Marie understood that they were all the masters of their own legs and arms, faces, hands, and feet. As if here, in the shower room, they'd found the way home to their bodies. To themselves.

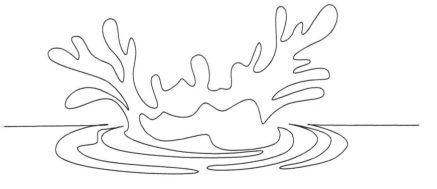

The Serpent Queen

"*Holy* crap!" Caroline screamed, and scrambled back into the air-conditioned house, slamming shut the sliding glass door to the patio. She should have had the presence of mind to soften her irreverent outburst to, say, simply, "Crap!" But in her terrible fright, she had not. For there—right on her new outdoor couch, sheltered from the rain by the cheerful turquoise-striped awning—lay the glossy, muscular coils of an enormous red snake.

The Homeowners' Association did not respond to Caroline's frantic phone calls for help.

She dialed 911.

"Could you describe the snake, ma'am?" the operator asked.

Caroline peeked outside. The reptile gazed placidly across the yard. "It's red, and . . . it's . . . huge! At least ten feet long!" Ten feet might have been an exaggeration, but she wanted them to understand that this was an emergency!

"Most likely a rat snake, ma'am. They're harmless. They live in holes in gardens and eat mice, toads. All this rain probably flooded the poor guy's den. You might want to keep that patio door shut so the slippery fella doesn't decide to come into the house."

Come into the house!?

"You need to send someone out here immediately to get rid of it!"

"Sorry, ma'am, but 911 doesn't handle animal pests. Have a nice day!"

Caroline stamped her foot and threw her cellphone at the recliner in the living room. A large red snake on her patio couch was intolerable! Someone had to get rid of this creature.

She could call her husband, Jim, but he wouldn't appreciate being disturbed in the middle of his Bible conference in Orlando. And anyway, what could he do from there?

Jim served as executive pastor at the You Deserve Your Reward Church in New Life, Florida, just west of Palm Beach. Every Sunday morning, he propelled himself onto the altar of the cavernous YDYR church—a former Target superstore—to inspire hundreds of the faithful with his impassioned sermons.

Coincidentally, the previous Sunday, he'd preached the story of Adam and Eve and the temptation of the serpent. And for no reason she could think of, Caroline had become annoyed and walked out of church early. Yes, she understood that the biblical passage about the serpent was meant to illustrate the importance of obedience to God. Still, she resented the idea that because Eve—a wife—had dared to ask questions, express curiosity, she'd become the villain of the story.

What if it had been Adam who'd chosen something scary and new? Just think of it: a man taking the initiative to eat a fruit or vegetable he had never tried before! *He'd probably be considered a hero*, she grumbled to herself.

Maybe her unpleasant serpentine visitor just wanted to get out of the rain, Caroline considered, as she watched it curled up quietly on the couch. It certainly didn't seem particularly . . . diabolical. Or inclined to slither off of the cushions and into her living room. She'd simply been shocked to be confronted with a large, animate, nonhuman presence. *Something actually lives out there*, she mused.

Jim and Caroline and their two kids had moved from dreary Michigan ten years earlier to Palazzo Splendido in New Life, Florida. Caroline could still remember how her heart had raced at the grandeur and perfection of the gated community. Everything made her feel special, chosen: the gleaming countertops and appliances; the pristine painted rooms that had never been occupied, and so held no trace of another family's quarrels, tantrums, or failures.

She wasn't sure when it had occurred to her that there were no birds.

"What would they eat?" a neighbor had pointed out when Caroline mentioned it. "Bird feeders are not allowed, and there are no insects, thank God. The neighborhood association takes care of that with weekly pesticide spraying."

In fact, aside from the occasional darting lizard, Caroline had never seen signs of another living creature. Until this big red snake showed up.

The snake twisted its neck around and gazed up at Caroline with eyes like jewels. A delicate, ribbon-thin tongue flicked in and out of its serpent mouth, which seemed almost to be turned up in a sly smile.

Intrigued, Caroline cautiously slid open the glass door and stepped outside.

Who you believe you are now is an illusion.

What? That strange thought, unconnected to anything, unfurled like a flower in her mind.

Caroline felt as if she were hallucinating—or entering a dream in which she observed herself from a distance. In this dream, the Caroline she saw appeared two-dimensional, like a character on the big flat-screen TV in their living room. Tears filled her eyes. How small and pathetic this version of herself seemed! An anxious, insignificant person who spent her days in shopping malls, exercise class, and trying with limited success to satisfy the demands of her husband and children.

Suddenly, the unhappy picture in her head blurred. No—that wasn't it. The picture was clear, but inside this vision, small, pathetic Caroline was blurred and rumpled. And more astonishingly, she actually began to split open like an old, worn, faded skin. What emerged from this husk was another creature altogether.

This new creature was still Caroline, but almost unrecognizable to herself: younger, glowing with strength and hope; but also older, larger, and more powerful, with none of her usual uncertainties or need to please. A frightening but thrilling energy seemed to emanate from this Caroline. The energy was like sex—though not sex as she had ever experienced it, but rapturous and potent. Could this Caroline really be her?

She began to see through the eyes of this new Caroline, and everything around her glittered with light and flashed with brilliant, intense color. In her mind, she could feel the texture of grass, the bark of trees, the soft, moist petals of flowers; she inhaled and perceived the thick luscious scents that roiled the air, and the sensory smorgasbord filled her with ecstasy.

Inside this awe-filled dream she thought she could hear the snake whispering:

You could be my queen . . .

As quickly and unexpectedly as it had entered her mind, the vision disappeared. Caroline slumped, holding on to the door frame for support.

On the patio couch, the snake coiled itself loosely and watched her.

"Mom, why are we stopping? Tyler and Lexington are coming over to play *Commando* on Xbox. I told them I'd be home at four."

Caroline glanced in the rearview mirror of her large minivan at the completely blank face of her teenage son as he stared at his cell phone. His thumbs twitched mechanically as he played a mobile game. Beside him in the backseat, Caroline's daughter, Madison, looked unhappy as she studied her own phone in its pink case. Her daughter rarely got together with her friends "IRL," as she would put it. Instead, they texted brief emoji-filled messages and compared altered and enhanced photos of one another.

She turned south onto Highway 441, a shimmering asphalt dividing line between the man-made wonders of Palazzo Splendido and the unruly landscape that led eventually to the Florida Everglades. Rough, sunburnt men and women wearing faded workshirts and rumpled jeans parked by the side of the road and sold things from their pick-up trucks—watermelons, strawberries, flowers.

Caroline pulled onto the shoulder beside a truck with the word *Orchids* painted along its side.

"I'll just be a minute," she said.

"Leave the a/c on," Zach said, his eyes never leaving his phone.

The wet heat enveloped Caroline as she emerged from the car, and her eyes met those of a wrinkled old woman who sat in a folding chair. Beside the woman, a plank tabletop held a lush array of orchids. Caroline had little interest in plants or flowers, except as hedges delineating their property from their neighbors'. But . . . there was something about orchids. Their blossoms were so unique and expressive, some even like the faces of small elves, while others provoked and excited Caroline's senses in a strange way.

As she bent over the plants, her attention was drawn to one with a frilly cascade of purple blossoms and thick, moist petals.

"You like?" the old woman asked.

"No. Well, yes . . . but it seems a little . . . too purple," she said. The thing was luscious and embarrassingly extravagant. Jim would probably hate it. "You know what? I'll take it."

"There are many more, where I live," the old woman said. "In my garden." She held a card, worn at the edges. The words *Lunaria's Garden* in purple ink twined around the design of a flower.

Lunaria.

Her hands felt soft and cool as she placed the card in Caroline's palm. "You are welcome to come."

As she was about to slip the card into her purse, Caroline noticed the printing on the reverse side: *Wild Animal Sanctuary.* After a sharp intake of breath, she said, "I have a snake . . . in my backyard."

Lunaria's eyes widened with interest but she said nothing.

"You understand . . . a, um, *serpiente*? It doesn't belong there. Where I live is . . . well, it's definitely not a good place for snakes. For any wild animals. But I can't get anyone to help me get rid of it. Do you, maybe, have a service or something? Someone who could remove the snake? I'm sure it would be much happier in a wild animal sanctuary."

"I will come," the old woman said. "One day this week."

Caroline exhaled with relief. "Let me give you my—"

"No need," Lunaria interjected. "My grandson is a gardener in that place where you live. He will find your house. He will know your car." She pointed at the eight-seat baby-blue mini-van with TVs in the headrests. It did stand out, Caroline had to admit, even among the many SUVs in Palazzo Splendido. The extra row of seats ensured that the vehicle took up at least two normal parking spaces.

"OK, well . . . thank you." With a small wave, acknowledged only by a faint smile, Caroline climbed back into her vehicle. Zach and Madison glanced up from their phones. "What's that?" Madison asked, pointing at the potted plant.

"A flower."

"Whatever," said Zach. "Can we go now?"

Two days later, on another rainy afternoon, Lunaria's truck pulled into Caroline's driveway, just as she ventured out of the controlled coolness of her house to gather the mail.

"Oh—hello!" she said as Lunaria climbed out of the truck and mounted the front steps ahead of her. "Please . . . come in," she managed, surprised at the old woman's vigor.

Since the day it had first appeared on Caroline's patio, the snake had made a regular habit of arriving midmorning and undulating its considerable length up onto the couch. At first, each of its visits had terrified Caroline; then they had just come to annoy her. The scaly thing had commandeered her own favorite spot, where she liked to relax with a cup of coffee once the kids were at school, Jim at work, and she had the house to herself.

"Did you bring a cage or a net or something?" Caroline asked Lunaria as she slid open the glass door to the backyard patio. The two women stepped out and regarded the thick red loops of the snake, upon which rested its oblong head. The snake's eyes were covered with pale, translucent lids; it appeared to be sleeping.

"I use my own method. Better."

Does she plan to kill it? Caroline wondered with a shiver. She hoped not—but she stayed quiet. Maybe it was best not to ask too many questions.

The old woman stood still for a moment, as if listening to something. Then, she sat down beside the snake.

Lazily, the snake blinked revealing topaz eyes and lifted its head, its coils loosening as it gazed at Lunaria. For what seemed a very long time, the two stared at each other.

"You must complete three tasks," said Lunaria, looking up at Caroline at last.

"What . . . tasks?"

"First, you must sing to him."

"Him? The snake?"

"Next, you must dance—like this." The old woman stood and undulated her ample lower body. Caroline had to stop herself from laughing at the absurdity of it.

"And third, you must sleep beside him."

"I am definitely NOT doing that."

"This is my advice to you," Lunaria said with finality, moving toward the glass slider. "It is the best method to make him go. Good luck."

"Wait. I thought you were going to—"

But the old woman was already disappearing through the front door. Before Caroline could catch up to her, Lunaria and her truck had vanished from the driveway.

After locking up behind her, Caroline walked back to the patio and stared at the unperturbed reptile. "Damn you," she muttered. Then, "Oh . . . what the heck." She perched gingerly at the far end of the couch.

The snake didn't move.

Self-consciously at first, quietly, Caroline began to hum. As a little girl, she had liked to sing made-up songs, as if the simple joy of being alive had to find a way to express itself. How different it felt to be an adult. Adult life—or hers, anyway—was rigid, anxiety provoking, and joyless, despite her beautiful house and all the beautiful new things she'd filled it with.

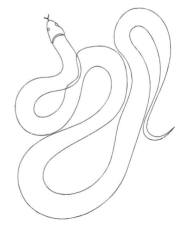

Gradually, her humming became a little bolder, more melodic. She allowed herself to slip into a happy daydream, singing and singing phrases from songs that came into her mind.

A peculiar sensation shook her with a start. To her horror, the snake had silently unwound some of his length, slid toward her, and laid his head in her lap!

She froze as the snake lifted his head and gazed up at her. As a child, Caroline hadn't been afraid of much—certainly not snakes. She could even remember holding one once, at a nature center. Its skin had been smooth to the touch, its body muscular. Stroking it, she'd felt fearless.

Perhaps the memory of brave, unselfconscious childhood is what inspired Caroline to slide out from under the creature, stand, and begin dancing for the snake. Her tentative little-girl movements soon gave way to slow, arching undulations.

With a preternatural majesty, his eyes never leaving hers, the big snake arched up his head and body. He began to move with Caroline, mirroring her slow, winding gestures until serpent and woman curved and twisted in a harmonious, silent dance.

A breeze moved through the leaves of the palm trees. Caroline's imagination traveled off to the west, where silver dolphins swam in the sapphire waterways of the Everglades and golden butterflies dipped in and out of the shadows. A flock of egrets, luminescent as opals, passed overhead on their way to the sea. As the ruby coils of the serpent rose and sank, twisted and turned, Caroline's mind was filled with the beauty of the living, breathing earth.

See? You haven't forgotten how beautiful it is.

Yes. She remembered now.

The sun rose in the sky. Noon came and went.

It was time to pick up the kids from school.

"We thank you for this bountiful feast which we, your unworthy children, are about to enjoy. Ah-men."

Jim had returned from his trip to Orlando and the family sat at the dinner table, eyes closed, as he led them in grace. Rain pelted the windows and sliding glass door. Zach and Madison were silent and withdrawn. The "no phones at the dinner table" rule was supposed to have encouraged family conversation. In reality it simply prompted the kids to eat at breakneck speed so they could vanish upstairs to their rooms, where their devices awaited them.

Caroline and Jim sat in awkward silence. Jim seemed as anxious as the kids to get up from the table. "It was quite a busy week," he said. "I've got a lot of catching-up to do."

She understood this to be his usual prelude to slipping off into his den to sit down in front of his email and catch his favorite online news segments, in which people shouted self-righteously at each other. She didn't try to stop him. In fact, she felt strangely detached, removing the rest of the dishes from the table and filling the dishwasher. Instead of replaying their conversation and wondering if she had said something wrong, she poured herself a glass of wine.

For once, she found herself uninterested in figuring out her husband's moods or nagging the kids about their sullen behavior. So what if they all insisted on hunkering down in their respective rooms with their respective electronics? Caroline pulled open the slider on the off chance that the snake might be in his spot on the couch. She imagined sitting beside him companionably, with her glass of wine. But the cushion was unoccupied and the rain showed no sign of letting up.

At bedtime, Caroline slid beneath the covers next to Jim without her nightgown on. He'd brought his laptop to bed and his face glowed blue in the reflection of the screen as he scrolled through emails.

"Oh," he said, feeling her next to him. "Hmmm. That's nice." Then, as if hesitant or unwilling to respond further to her warm body, he pointed to the nightstand. "New plant?" he asked.

"It's an orchid," she said. Its luxuriant purple flowers seemed to pulse with her own sudden and inexplicable sexual yearning.

"It looks a little ghoulish, doesn't it?" said Jim. "Honestly, I think those silk flowers you have around the house are prettier. Easier to take care of, too."

He went back to scrolling, clicking, filing, deleting. "I didn't have much time to work on my sermon during the conference," he said. "You know, with the biblical workshops and networking."

"Why don't you put that thing away now," she whispered. An itchy, sexy feeling had taken hold of her, banishing her usual feeling of being too tired, or fat. She kissed her husband's cheek and snuggled against him, but he didn't respond. At last, Caroline fell asleep to the sound of his fingers still tapping away at the keyboard.

In the middle of the night, she found herself wide awake. Jim, unconscious and snoring, was slumped over the laptop, which had gone dark. She wrapped herself in her fluffy pink bathrobe, then crossed the bedroom in her bare feet, stopping for a moment outside the closed doors of each of her children's rooms. She hesitated, imagining her children's faces, their soft breathing.

Quietly, she crept down the stairs and out onto the back patio. The rain had tapered off and a few stars twinkled in the night sky; even the moon was visible, despite the glow of the development and the nearby mall. Once, she'd found it comforting to know that there were lots of people out there, all around her. But now she missed the darkness. It had been so long since she'd experienced night as it was meant to be, lit only by the moon and stars.

Even just a few days ago, Caroline would have said she preferred to be inside, where environmental conditions were steady and controlled. But tonight, the air in the yard felt pleasant, almost liquid, as if she'd slipped into a pool or lagoon. How nice it might be to sleep outside, she thought, as she curled sideways on the couch and then stretched out across the cushions.

Come with me. Leave all this and be mine. . . .

In her dream the serpent had returned and was lying beside her on the couch. She knew she was dreaming because there was no way, in real life, she would be sleeping with a snake. Her mind drifted to something she had wanted to tell Jim: He had gotten it wrong—they both had.

She understood now, and wanted to tell him that it was not the serpent who had led them out of the garden. The temptation they'd succumbed to was from all the beautiful, shiny new things to look at and to buy that in the end never seemed to satisfy. Things that clicked and whirred irresistibly, and seemed to promise to make those who touched them feel new, too.

It was a temptation they had created—and fallen for—all by themselves.

"CAROLINE! OH, MY GOD!"

She sat bolt upright, disoriented and shaken at the sound of Jim's voice. A light drizzle fell from a pale gray sky. It was not yet morning.

"What, Jim? What is it?"

"Do not move a muscle, do you hear me, Caroline? I'll be right back."

Caroline blinked, and then she realized what had caused his alarm. Beside her on the couch lay the snake, gazing at her with sleepy eyes, and oddly, she felt no fear of him. The snake felt smooth and warm beneath her fingers as she reached out to stroke his long, scaled body. Why did Jim have to make such a fuss?

Jim returned to the patio with a rifle. Zach and Madison pushed through the slider behind him, rubbing sleep from their eyes. Though he was a man of God, Jim knew his Second Amendment rights, and the fact that a homeowner facing an intruder had every right to shoot first and ask questions later.

"Jim! Oh, my God, Jim—are you insane?" shouted Caroline.

"Get out of the way, Caroline!" Jim ordered, leveling the .22.

"Disgusting!" cried Madison. "We have GOT to move out of this place!"

"Shoot it, Dad!" Zach yelled, squeezing behind his father and aiming his phone camera at the couch. "Kill it!"

"Your father will do no such thing! Jim—put the gun down."

In all the commotion, the snake slid soundlessly off the couch and toward the shelter of the backyard shrubs. Seeing that the snake was out of range of his wife, Jim aimed and took his shot.

The impact threw the snake up into the air. The wounded animal landed with a sickly thud.

"JIM! What have you done?!" Caroline cried.

Caroline ran to the still body of the snake and fell to her knees beside him. The shot had hit squarely, nearly severing a foot of length from the snake's tail end. She laid her hands on the snake's body and the animal shuddered. His beautiful eyes had already begun to cloud over. Caroline thought her heart would break.

She knew what she had to do. She gathered the limp and heavy creature in her arms and stumbled past her astonished family. Still in her pink bathrobe, she grabbed her purse and keys and headed for the minivan, where she gently laid the bloody snake on the passenger seat. She floored the gas pedal and tore out of the cul-de-sac, sending torrents of rainwater onto the curb.

Caroline sped up 441 to Okeechobee Boulevard, then turned west past miles of chain restaurants and big-box superstores. As the landscape became more rural and wild, she slowed the car and fumbled in her purse for the old woman's card—but before she could put her hands on it, she saw a sign with an arrow pointing at a narrow dirt track that cut through dense undergrowth: *Lunaria's Garden.*

She swerved onto the track and maneuvered her large vehicle through the tangle of smooth branches and palm fronds. Oak trees with hanging moss towered over her. When she glanced in the rearview mirror, it seemed as if the jungle had closed in behind her, cutting her off from the world she knew.

The last pale sliver of the crescent moon reclined low in the brightening dawn sky. Beneath it, a small cottage came into view. Caroline rolled down her window and called, "Help! I need help!"

A light went on in the front window and a young man emerged from the cottage. "What do you want here, lady?" he asked.

"Your grandmother, is she here? I need her help. I have an injured animal. A snake." Caroline got out of the car and ran around to the passenger side, where the young man joined her. His face darkened when she opened the passenger door. Gently, he lifted and cradled the limp, smooth creature.

"Is he . . . still alive?" stammered Caroline.

"We will see," said the boy. "Follow me." He carried the snake into the house as Caroline stumbled after him, tears streaming down her face.

"*¡La serpiente está herida!*" shouted the young man.

Seated in front of a small wood-burning stove, the old woman looked up from the glowing embers. "Just as I expected," she muttered, "*lo sabía*. I knew there would be trouble." Caroline followed the old woman and the young man carrying the snake out through the rear of the house to the back garden.

There she stopped, gaping in wonder. The morning light spilled into the small clearing, illuminating the ancient, many-limbed trees, hundreds of which seemed to extend far back into the shadows. Flowers were everywhere: in pots and baskets, tucked into the limbs of trees. Birds were flitting through the trees—so many birds. As she stood quietly, she thought she could feel the whole garden breathing—the trees, plants, darting lizards, even the rocks and the small stream that trickled along the pathway were all softly inhaling, then exhaling, a healing perfume.

Blood oozed from the snake's wound. Setting the snake on a low, stone table, the old woman pulled out a sharp knife and sliced off the bloodied portion of the creature's tail with a swift stroke. From a pocket of her dress, she extracted some fine black thread and a needle, and quickly sewed up the wound. Not sure how she could help, Caroline moved out of the way and settled into a hammock strung between two thick palm trunks.

"He is weak but alive," said Lunaria. "Now, he needs warmth." Carefully, she lifted the heavy creature into her arms. "He has many talents, this serpent, as I think you know by now. But he cannot make his own warmth."

"My husband saw him on the couch next to me and—before I could stop him—he got his gun and . . ." Caroline buried her face in her hands. "It's all my fault really," she said in a hoarse whisper.

"There is no use crying about the past. There is only now. You must decide what you want to do."

"What do you mean?"

"You can save the serpent, but it will not be easy."

"What must I do?"

"You must give up your old life: your husband and children, your house . . . even this body. Everything."

It was crazy. Unthinkable. But, somehow . . . Caroline understood it to be what she desired.

She began to weep for the loss of her illusions, her plans, and her certainties about everything—including herself. What kind of a wife would leave her husband? What kind of a mother would leave her children? But even as one part of her heart revolted, another part was already separating itself from all she'd held close. Jim would be content without her in time, like a frog in his little pond, surrounded by his followers. Her children, who were already moving away from her, would continue forward into the clamor of their adult lives and experiences.

"Dream about it," said Lunaria. She placed the wounded snake beside Caroline in the hammock, and disappeared.

The serpent stirred, undulating itself beneath the folds of Caroline's bathrobe to gather her warmth. She trembled but forced herself to remain still. Gradually, the creature wound his body around hers, up and up her torso and around her neck. When she felt the swooning delight of the serpent's tongue across her face and lips—*love's first kiss*—every memory of houses and clothes and shopping malls dissolved and all that existed was the living, breathing forest around her and the animal beside her.

See?

She did see. She saw how beautiful the light was as it played through the trees, how elegant and perfect the hummingbird darting among the dark leaves and bright flowers. She heard the music of flowing water; the soft whispering of creatures moving through the shadows. There was living, and dying too, she understood, as each individual sprang forth, blossomed, then faded and merged into the greater harmony of all beings. Above all, she felt a vast contentment.

The great tenderness of the serpent consumed Caroline and she was transformed, becoming long and smooth herself, glowing with strength and vitality. Everything she could see and feel—the plants and animals, the breeze against her skin, the scent of damp earth—it had all been here always, all around her. But she had been as dull as a block of concrete, as remote from an actual living being as an image on a computer screen. She'd been unable to perceive any of it. Until now.

I've chosen. And she entwined her long sinuous length with that of the serpent king.

In the days that followed, the rain continued, making many of the streets impassable. Lunaria's grandson took the minivan back to Palazzo Splendido, where big, shiny machines belong. Someday, Lunaria said, maybe soon, all of the houses, stores, restaurants—everything made by man—would wash away. The slow, pulsing movement of water through the Everglades would return, and the deep flowing river of grass would flourish again.

In the meantime, Lunaria would tend her garden, with its exuberant flowers and shadowy creatures. The old woman felt it was only right to congratulate herself: Not only had she succeeded in retrieving the obstinate snake from Palazzo Splendido—removing him, as she'd promised—but she had added a new creature to her garden. Where there had once been only one serpent, now there were two . . . though one of them had a tail that was just a foot shorter.

The Gardener

Their neighbor stops over to say goodbye. He and his family have been renting the farmhouse next to their white vacation cottage in Maine.

Although she hasn't met him, she's seen the neighbor and his daughter walking down the path to the lake, like a vision of herself as a child dancing through a summer field beside her own father. Both her parents are dead now, but those long-ago summers when she took for granted the unchanging circle of her family remain vivid in her memory.

He opens the trunk of his car. "I thought you might want the firewood we didn't use." It's kind of him. Their fireplace provides the only heat for the cottage and the October nights have grown chilly. He helps her boyfriend and her stack the logs in their woodshed.

"You're heading home?" her boyfriend asks when they finish. The neighbor leans against the side of his car.

"Yes, back to Brooklyn. Then Colombia, where my wife is from. We've been here since March, since the coronavirus lockdown started. My wife wants to see her family. I'm not sure when we'll return to the US. A lot depends upon the political situation."

Once, she might have thought this comment referred to Colombia. But he's talking about the United States. The unspoken question passes between the three of them: *Is the America we grew up in lost?*

"Since March? Lucky!" She changes the subject. They had taken off from Colorado in mid-September. They drove across the country in three days, car strapped down with a kayak and bikes. Just get to Maine.

"I wanted my family out of New York. I found some landscaping work here on the island, but that's over for the season." He looks toward the hills that darken beneath the evening sky. "It's beautiful here. I wish we didn't have to leave."

"Did you build that circular fence, with the garden inside?" She can't help noticing, every time she walks by the farmhouse, the intricate enclosure woven as if by magic from fallen branches.

He nods. "There's still a lot of parsley and basil in there. Help yourself. It would make me happy if you could use some of those herbs." He asks, "If I gave you my email address, would you send me a picture of the trees, when the leaves change color? I'm sorry to miss that." He is very thin, and with such sorrowful eyes.

A few days after he and his family have gone, she types his name into a Google search. There he is, fifteen years ago, featured in *Art in America* for a mammoth environmental art project in Colombia. Other reviews mention installations in New York. For a moment, he captured the public's enthusiasm. Then that attention slipped loose, it seems to her, and moved on.

Misty rain hangs in the air the next morning as she strolls over to the garden and steps inside the circle as enchanting as a faerie ring. Here grows the lushest parsley with the largest leaves she has ever seen. Basil, green and purple. Masses of pungent sage that come to her knees. Vines with small tomatoes twisting between the branch fencing. Blue-flowered burdock, golden nasturtiums.

It is a kind of beauty that makes her want to drop to her knees and weep. How could he have made this—something so beautiful, so evident of care—knowing he would have to leave it?

Ten days later the leaves reach their peak. Riding their mountain bikes, she and her boyfriend race along the quiet carriage paths as if swimming in color—waves of purple, scarlet, gold, and swells of green pines. On a deserted stretch of beach, they peel off their clothes and dash into the freezing water. She is a child again—they both are—shrieking with laughter, exhilarated.

Returning to the cottage, she stops to take a photo of the circular garden with the hillside and mountains in the distance. She sends that picture with the leaves on the hill, all a riot of vivid colors, at their moment of glory.

Maybe what their neighbor, the artist and gardener, had already come to terms with is that you lose everything. And so you try to make beauty—or at least you try to see it—along the way. Maybe beauty is what makes all the loss that comes, sooner or later, bearable.

That night a cold wind sweeps in. They light a fire in the fireplace with the neighbor's gift of wood. The next day it rains, hard, and the leaves begin to fall.

Returning

She pushes off from the beach, steadying herself as the canoe glides through the water. On the opposite shore sits the lake house, patient as stone.

The girl she once was, all skinned knees and elbows, runs from house to shore to meet her middle-aged self. Before her parents died. Before their house was sold to strangers.

Bare feet step into the shallows, seeking solid ground. How long has she wished for the day the usurping strangers, too, would succumb to the passage of time, death, or family dispersing?

She's waited all these years. To climb the steep path, the wide stairs, to stand before the front door in which—*there*—reflected in the glass panes she sees the girl she left behind.

A board creaks underfoot. She bends to find the old keys in their hiding place. They jangle between her fingers—playing memory's distant music.

The Land Owner's Daughter

"Hill Top is *unique*," Elise asserted, smacking the desk with the flat of her hand. "The way the property lies high up above the town, above all the neighboring farms. And the views of the Blue Ridge Mountains—nothing compares!"

"It certainly is a beautiful place," Wyatt agreed.

"Over one thousand acres! It took my father fifty years to buy all the land. He devoted his life to this property. Imagine!" Her words spilled out in a strident jumble. "And the house—you've seen it, you know—it's a Victorian masterpiece."

"Yes. Yes, indeed."

She got to her point. "I'm the only one of my siblings who cares. I'm the only one who *honors the property* the way my parents would have wanted. I need your help, Wyatt. Now that my parents are both dead, Hill Top should be mine!"

Elise abruptly stood and marched out of the attorney's office, leaving maps, deeds, scribbled notes, and a department store receipt for several pairs of shoes scattered across his desk.

As the only lawyer in the small Virginia farming town, Wyatt had been engaged over the years by Elise's father to handle the gradual acquisition, parcel by parcel, of those one thousand acres. The politically prominent family had lived in Washington, DC, and spent summers and winter holidays at the Hill Top estate. In their later years, Elise's parents had permanently moved to the grand Victorian farmhouse, before ending their days in a nursing home.

Early on, Wyatt had fallen for Elise. He'd been an ambitious young man: soft-spoken but determined, and committed to daily weight lifting in his garage. Elise had seemed to him as dazzling and perfect as an angel, with her waves of long chestnut hair and fine features, and the sparkle of her laughter as the world arranged itself to please her.

Despite his comparatively low social status, young Wyatt had convinced himself that he had a chance with this captivating girl—and her imposing father had allowed the impression that he approved. Boldly, he'd once invited her to see a movie in town. He still remembered—all these years later—the shame he'd felt at the amused look on her face.

"*Wyatt*," she chided the awkward and skinny young man from town, "you can't be serious?"

He decided to drive up to Hill Top that evening with the papers she'd left behind. Though he would never admit it, he felt compelled to test himself, to gauge his reaction yet again to this once longed-for prize.

Before today, Wyatt hadn't seen Elise in at least twenty years. This morning in his office he'd been shocked, frankly, at the spectacle of the frenzied septuagenarian with her oddly disjointed speech, her bag spilling folders and indecipherable notes. Deep furrows punctuated her brow, and her mouth twitched with suspicion. Time and life's disappointments had smudged Elise's exquisite beauty.

Wyatt had had his disappointments, too. His brief marriage had fizzled when his wife took exception to his long work hours—much of which had been spent on matters pertaining to Elise's family. But there had been so many successful property deals, each concluding with an invitation to Hill Top for champagne. *Champagne.* No one else Wyatt knew drank champagne.

As the years went by, Wyatt had prospered. His waistline had expanded, and so had his office, his home, and his collection of tweed blazers befitting a successful country lawyer. For his sixty-fifth birthday, he'd bought himself a Porsche convertible. In a town so small no traffic light impeded his passage, Wyatt imagined he made quite an impression as he veered past the tractors, pickup trucks, and nondescript clunkers.

Elise, he'd learned from their brief meeting, had spent her youth and middle age in Georgetown society circles, waiting, he surmised, for a suitable matrimonial offer. In the end, she'd never married.

Now, there was something she needed from *him*. Perhaps the scales had tipped.

After a thirty-minute drive, Wyatt turned his Porsche into the long driveway and parked in front of the house. On impulse, rather than heading directly to the front door, he walked over to where light shone through low-set windows. He peered in, noting absently that the trim could really use a coat of paint.

Elise was pacing in front of a wide hearth where a fire blazed beneath the ornate mantel. She smoked a cigarette and clutched a full glass of wine—clearly from the box that sat on a bench beside the hearth. The cheap, supermarket beverage clashed with the refined image he'd held of her. Elise appeared to be shouting at someone, but as far as he could tell no one but she occupied the room.

He returned to the front door, knocked, and was greeted with an angry diatribe.

"I haven't been able to get hold of the caretaker—he's avoiding my calls—and I'm *so upset*! It's very important that the swimming pond continue to be stocked with trout and that the petunias in the hanging baskets along the porch not be neglected. I can't do everything!"

"No, you can't," Wyatt agreed, following her inside.

To his surprise, he couldn't help pitying Elise. Perhaps he alone shared with her the memory of a youthful glamour and family fortune that had once inspired those around her to comply at once with her every wish.

"It's been up to me, these past five years. *I* was the one who drove from Georgetown each month to make certain that standards were maintained and the house was properly kept up, while Mother and Daddy went *on and on* in the nursing home. All my brother and sister ever did was complain about the expense. And now that both our parents are gone, they want to sell!"

She paused for breath and another gulp of wine, giving Wyatt a chance to glance around. The mention of standards forced him to notice how run down—dirty, even—the house appeared. Did these rooms, in Elise's mind, still shimmer with those long-ago weekends when important guests would come to stay—writers, politicians, even the occasional film star? When there was horseback riding and swimming, the soft *shush* of her mother's expensive dresses and cocktail parties that went on until dawn?

"My brother has cancer—or *so he says.* My sister lives in London. It doesn't matter to her that this place represents our parents' life's work. They're both so selfish!

"The real problem, Wyatt, is that Mother and Daddy *just lived too damn long.* They went through my entire inheritance! All I have left is this house and the property."

"According to the will, you and your brother and sister are *equal* beneficiaries."

"*Technically.*" She emptied what was left of the wine into her glass. "But I'm the only one who cares about Hill Top. It should go to me! They don't deserve it. I intend," she asserted with a self-deluding grandiosity that Wyatt found oddly impressive, "to make certain this estate continues to be run the way our parents would have wanted."

She marched toward the kitchen, her shrill, angry voice rising and falling as she scavenged, Wyatt guessed, for another box of wine. Elise returned to the living room empty-handed. "I need to get hold of that caretaker about the trout!" She burst into tears. "The pond must be stocked with trout!"

A few days later, Wyatt and Elise met in his office again to review the will. "I just want you to be prepared, Elise," he said evenly. "We will likely have to find some way to settle with your siblings."

"No! They have *no right* to our parents' possessions." Her face contorted, then shifted into a conspiratorial smirk. "I found a drawer full of love letters my parents sent to each other after they became engaged. I plan to burn them."

"*Burn* them?"

"In their honor. So that no one else can ever read them. Certainly not my sister and brother."

The idea of Elise with a flaming cache of letters alarmed Wyatt more than the legal ramifications of destroying jointly held property. "Why don't you hold off on . . . disposing of any articles in the house for now," he said firmly. He knew he had to take charge of the situation—and of Elise. "I'm doing my best to sort things out for you."

"I knew I could count on you, Wyatt." Her eyes shone with the charm of a girl.

In spite of himself, his heart lurched.

He drove up to the property that evening, uncertain of his motive. Was it pure lawyerly concern or something else? Thunder murmured in the darkening sky and he closed the top on the convertible. How many times had he traveled this road, his pulse quickening, drawn irresistibly by the vision of a place as remote from his daily life as Camelot?

Still some distance from Hill Top, he smelled smoke.

The Porsche screeched up the driveway. Wyatt jumped out and rushed to the house. Finding the front door locked, he heaved open a downstairs window and scrambled through.

Elise stood in the center of the living room, the burning letters fluttering about the fireplace, drifting all around her. Where the charred sheets landed, the threadbare oriental rug ignited and flames raced across the rug and up the curtains. The conflagration would soon block any means of escape.

"Let it burn!" sobbed Elise. She struggled as Wyatt wrestled her into his arms and dragged her away from the flames and toward the gaping window. A flash of lightning snaked across the sky and the air sizzled as rain began to tumble out of storm-blackened clouds. "Everything that matters is gone. No one cares but me!"

Hoisting her writhing form over the low windowsill to safety and then following, he hollered, "*I care!*" From a place of terrible, reckless longing, the words sprang to his lips before he could stop them.

"You don't! How can you?" In her grief, she rebuffed him. "I'm so alone!"

"No, you're not, Elise!"

Wyatt reeled as she flailed at him with her fists and then—with a theatrical moan—collapsed into his arms. Drenched and shaking, clutching Elise to his chest, Wyatt refused to concede that he was far too old for this sort of drama.

Instead, as the fire crept through the open window and began to lick at the brittle frames, he knew he would not abandon her. Could not.

All his quiet and circumspect life Wyatt had looked up the hill toward this house, with its one thousand acres and the beautiful girl who had long ago turned him down. It was too late! he understood, as he held Elise in his embrace. It was too late, now, to give up wanting what once he thought he could not have.

Leaving New York

Jack kneels at her feet in the resort lobby, adjusting her ski boot buckles.

Bundled in layers of unfamiliar mountain gear, Rachel tries to catch her breath in the thin-aired, sharp-peaked realm of snow and ice. She looks down at the wide shoulders and the muscular thighs that belong to a man who was once the boy who gave her rides on the back of his bike in summer. She and Jack had traded silly notes in classes; in winter he'd pelted her with snowballs. He had always been her best friend.

As a young woman, Rachel remembers, she'd held all the cards, commanded the advantage. Now, like a middle-aged version of Cinderella, she struggles to put on her game face while Jack buckles her feet into the heavy rental ski boots. The boots will attach to the two fiberglass planks on which she has agreed to be propelled into the terrifying unknown.

All around the ski lodge, boisterous groups of athletic jet-setters greet one another before a day on the slopes. She notices a woman in a slim white ski suit, with taut Nordic beauty and a high-pitched voice drawing the attention of an elegant flock of friends. The woman pauses to run her gaze over Rachel's borrowed ski pants and down parka. Then she turns back to her companions, laughing gaily.

At the gourmet breakfast bar, handsome young men serve up flirtatious banter and frothy cappuccinos. The familiar aroma of coffee fills Rachel with a desire to retreat to a comfortable chair by the picture window and throw in the towel. What if she suggests that Jack go on without her? He could join the aggressively cheerful crowd while she stays here, wrapped in the safe, warm smell of overpriced lattes and blueberry scones.

But that was the trouble—she'd always hesitated. *I can't leave New York*, she'd tell him. Her job was too important, or it might be, someday; or the timing wasn't right as another romantic interest distracted her. The city spun fantasies of cocktails and laughter, gallery openings, parties, and cab rides after midnight. It whispered that it was only here, in the crush of striving and ambition, where her dreams could be fulfilled.

Eventually Jack had stopped asking her and simply moved forward, his modest hopes and practical plans always lighting a clearer path for him. He'd driven his parents' old VW super-Beetle out west, found a job teaching skiing. And Rachel had stayed back east.

Where did she put her helmet? Her gloves? Her mouth is dry now, and sticky with fear. She anticipates her humiliation as Jack regrets inviting her to his rarefied world where sporty competence surely wins the day. Had he hoped she'd be more like the beautiful, chic woman jostling out the doors to the gondola with her entourage of friends?

One day—*how had so much time passed?*—Rachel had realized that everything just seemed to have gotten smaller. Her apartment, her work, the tiny office down on Varick Street with the window and a door that she'd once fought so hard for. Her life and her range of options, shrunken as the years had gone by.

"Okay! That should do it." Jack presses up off his knees and stands before her. He radiates uncomplicated warmth, and enthusiasm for the adventure ahead. "How does that feel, Rach?" In the muddle of Rachel's anxious-hopeful mind, the answer to that question becomes something about the sensation of his hands, how they felt even through the hard boots, the thick socks. Strong. Sure. Encouraging.

If he'd wanted someone else, he wouldn't have asked—again—for her to come. And despite being muffled beneath tectonic layers of fleece and thermal and all-weather engineered materials, Rachel can imagine exactly the sensation of being touched by him. Like snow

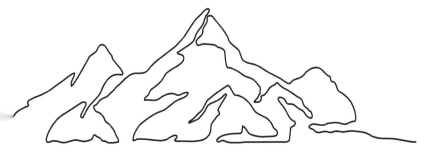

melting. Like forgiving herself, for all the wrong turns, detours, the time lost.

"I feel good!" she answers.

Jack pushes open the heavy doors for her, to a world of dizzying space where soaring white pinnacles press up against the blue-domed sky. "You ready to play in the snow?" his voice calls to her.

A gust of wind blows up a flurry of powder; the brilliant crystals catch and swirl all around them. She lifts her face to feel the cold sparks against her cheeks. There are many kinds of magic, after all.

Rachel stomps her heavy boots, and her smile meets his. "I'm ready."

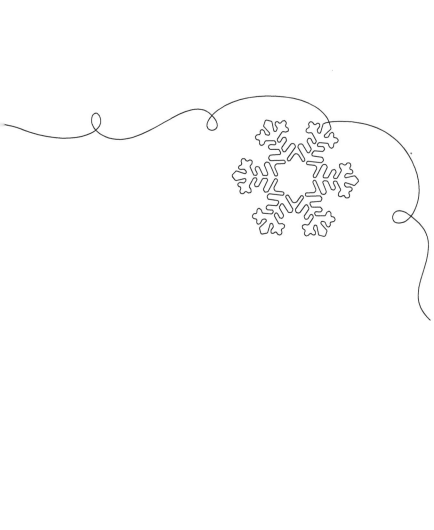

Author's Note and Thanks

With these stories I have tried to capture, as seen from my small corner of life, some of what it has felt like to be a woman in the late twentieth and early twenty-first centuries. One with a restless longing for love and experience, matched at times in equal measure by foolishness and a disregard for common sense.

These pieces came together over a three-year period, from 2019 to 2022. In writing them, I hoped to explore grief and loss; the fluid connections between humans and the natural world; above all, the strange forms love can take.

I am grateful to the talented readers who have reviewed these stories and offered thoughtful comments and suggestions. My editor, Laura Ross, has provided invaluable help with her many readings of the various rewrites of these stories; she never seems to tire of cheering me on when I need it most. Editor Ella Peary of Authors Publish has been an important friend, reader, and adviser for me, as have the members of my writers' group, Julian Woodruff, Becca Moore, Vali Hawkins Mitchell, and Kristen Baum DeBeasi. I had the good fortune to have my friend Jeff Deck of the New Hampshire Writers Project review and critique a number of these stories.

Pulling together this collection to create a beautiful book were Karen Wyatt, my friend and the publisher of Sunroom Studios; designer Ashley Prine of Tandem Books; copy editor Kate Griggs;

and proofreader Lisa Thornbloom. In collaborating with this team of women who did such an amazing job on my debut novel, I second editor Laura Ross's enthusiasm: "the band is back together again!"

Friends and family have offered feedback, encouragement, and hugs. Among these were childhood pals Jane Flynn, Désirée Elsevier, and Dorothy Kindred Yewer. And my niece Amanda Sater, also a wonderful reader, continues to surprise and inspire me from her vantage point of the next generation; she and my nieces Naomi Dulit-Greenberg and Sarah Feingold are as curious about life as I was and am, but as young women so much wiser in many ways.

Above all I am grateful for the love of my husband, Alan Dulit, that allows me to try to make something meaningful with words.

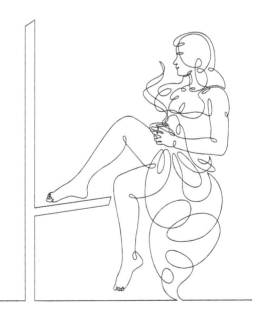

Acknowledgments

I thank the editors of the following publications in which several of these pieces have previously appeared, sometimes in a slightly different form:

"Commencement": *101words.org*, October 6, 2020

"Table for One": *BOMBFIRE*, September 25, 2021

"Thief": *Bright Flash Literary Review*, November 1, 2021

"Smoke": *Blue Lake Review*, January 2022

"The Swimming Pool": *BOMBFIRE*, April 24, 2021

"The Shower Room": *Muleskinner Journal*, November 2021

"The Serpent Queen": *Adelaide Literary Magazine*, July 20, 2020

"The Gardener": *The Forge Literary Magazine*, May 2, 2022

"Returning": *City.River.Tree*, June 16, 2021

"Leaving New York": *Potato Soup Journal*, Best of 2021 Anthology (March 2022)

About the Author

A native of New York and the White Mountains of New Hampshire, Christina Holbrook lived and worked in New York City for many years. Her work in the publishing and print production industries took her frequently to Europe and the Far East. She is married to Alan Dulit, and now calls Breckenridge, Colorado, home.

Holbrook's debut novel, *All the Flowers of the Mountain*, was published in 2022. Please visit www.christinaholbrook.com. You can follow her on Instagram at @christinaholbrookwrites.

Printed in the USA
CPSIA information can be obtained
at www.ICGtesting.com
CBHW041338120224
4282CB00024B/785